# DUEL WITH A SPACE PIRATE!

Lucky Starr, officer of the Council of Science, stared at the man who had challenged him to a duel. "What weapons? Or is it bare fists?"

"Weapons!" the huge lump of gristle replied, his eyes glittering. "Push-tubes! In open space!"

Lucky's heart plummeted. A push-gun duel required an expert. Fought by professionals, it was deadly! "I accept," he said.

*What else could he do? This man had helped to kill Lucky's parents!*

Fawcett Books by Isaac Asimov:

THE EARLY ASIMOV, *Book One*
THE EARLY ASIMOV, *Book Two*
PEBBLE IN THE SKY
THE STARS, LIKE DUST
THE CURRENTS OF SPACE
THE CAVES OF STEEL
THE END OF ETERNITY
I, ROBOT
THE MARTIAN WAY
THE NAKED SUN
EARTH IS ROOM ENOUGH
NINE TOMORROWS
NIGHTFALL
THE GODS THEMSELVES
THE BEST OF ISAAC ASIMOV
TALES OF THE BLACK WIDOWERS
MORE TALES OF THE BLACK WIDOWERS
THE BICENTENNIAL MAN AND OTHER STORIES

The Lucky Starr Series by Isaac Asimov:

DAVID STARR, SPACE RANGER
LUCKY STARR AND THE PIRATES OF THE ASTEROIDS
LUCKY STARR AND THE OCEANS OF VENUS
LUCKY STARR AND THE BIG SUN OF MERCURY
LUCKY STARR AND THE MOONS OF JUPITER
LUCKY STARR AND THE RINGS OF SATURN

And these anthologies edited by Isaac Asimov:

THE HUGO WINNERS, *Volume I*
STORIES FROM THE HUGO WINNERS, *Volume II*
MORE STORIES FROM THE HUGO WINNERS, *Volume III*
WHERE DO WE GO FROM HERE?
BEFORE THE GOLDEN AGE, *Book 1*
BEFORE THE GOLDEN AGE, *Book 2*
BEFORE THE GOLDEN AGE, *Book 3*

And non-fiction by Isaac Asimov:

EARTH: OUR CROWDED SPACESHIP
REALM OF ALGEBRA
REALM OF NUMBERS

# ISAAC ASIMOV

writing as Paul French

# LUCKY STARR

and

# THE PIRATES OF THE ASTEROIDS

FAWCETT CREST • NEW YORK

*LUCKY STARR AND THE PIRATES OF THE ASTEROIDS*

THIS BOOK CONTAINS THE COMPLETE TEXT OF THE ORIGINAL HARDCOVER EDITION.

Published by Fawcett Crest Books, a unit of CBS Publications, the Consumer Publishing Division of CBS Inc., by arrangement with Doubleday and Company, Inc.

ISBN: 0-449-23421-5

Printed in the United States of America

11   10   9   8   7   6   5   4   3   2

# CONTENTS

## DEDICATION

To Frederik Pohl,
That contradiction in terms—
A lovable agent.

# Preface

Back in the 1950s, I wrote a series of six derring-do novels about David "Lucky" Starr and his battles against malefactors within the Solar System. Each of the six took place in a different region of the system and in each case I made use of the astronomical facts—as they were then known.

Now, a quarter-century later, Fawcett is bringing out the novels in new editions; but what a quarter-century it has been! More has been learned about the worlds of our Solar System in this last quarter-century than in all the thousands of years of earlier observations.

Prior to the 1950s, you see, we could only look from Earth's surface; since then, we have been able to send out rocket probes to take photographs and make studies at close range.

The only one of the six Lucky Starr novels that has remained untouched by this—at least so far—is *LUCKY STARR AND THE PIRATES OF THE ASTEROIDS*, which was written in 1953. There is evidence that many of the asteroids may be a little darker and just a little larger than had been thought earlier, but that makes very little difference.

Therefore, Lucky can fight the pirates and engage in his deadly duels right now just as he did a quarter-

century ago, when this book was written. If I had to
write the novel today, I would hardly have to change
a word.

ISAAC ASIMOV

# 1

## The Doomed Ship

*Fifteen minutes to zero time!* The *Atlas* waited to take off. The sleek, burnished lines of the space-ship glittered in the bright Earthlight that filled the Moon's night sky. Its blunt prow pointed upward into empty space. Vacuum surrounded it and the dead pumice of the Moon's surface was under it. The number of its crew was zero. There wasn't a living person aboard.

Dr. Hector Conway, Chief Councilor of Science, said, "What time is it, Gus?"

He felt uncomfortable in the Moon offices of the Council. On Earth he would have been at the very top of the stone and steel needle they called Science Tower. He would have been able to look out the window toward International City.

Here on the Moon they did their best. The offices had mock windows with brilliantly designed Earth scenes behind them. They were colored naturally, and lights within them brightened and softened during the day, simulating morning, noon, and evening. During the sleep periods they even shone a dim, dark blue.

It wasn't enough, though, for an Earthman like Conway. He knew that if he broke through the glass of the windows there would be only painted miniatures before his eyes, and if he got behind that, then there would be just another room, or maybe the solid rock of the Moon.

Dr. Augustus Henree, whom Conway had addressed, looked at his wrist. He said, between puffs at his pipe, "There's still fifteen minutes. There's no point in worrying. The *Atlas* is in perfect shape. I checked it myself yesterday."

"I know that." Conway's hair was pure white and he looked older than the lank, thin-faced Henree, though they were the same age. He said, "It's Lucky I'm worried about."

"Lucky?"

Conway smiled sheepishly. "I'm catching the habit, I'm afraid. I'm talking about David Starr. It's just that everyone calls him Lucky these days. Haven't you heard them?"

"Lucky Starr, eh? The name suits him. But what about him? This is all his idea, after all."

"Exactly. It's the sort of idea he gets. I think he'll tackle the Sirian Consulate on the Moon next."

"I wish he would."

"Don't joke. Sometimes I think you encourage him in his idea that he ought to do everything as a one-man job. It's why I came here to the Moon, to keep an eye on him, not to watch the ship."

"If that's what you came here for, Hector, you're not on the job."

"Oh well, I can't follow him about like a mother

hen. But Bigman is with him. I told the little fellow I would skin him alive if Lucky decided to invade the Sirian Consulate singlehanded."

Henree laughed.

"I tell you he'd do it," grumbled Conway. "What's worse, he'd get away with it, of course."

"Well, then."

"It would just encourage him, and then someday he'll take one risk too many, and he's too valuable a man to lose!"

John Bigman Jones teetered across the packed clay flooring, carrying his stein of beer with the utmost care. They didn't extend the pseudo-gravity fields outside the city itself, so that out here at the space-port you had to do the best you could under the Moon's own gravity field. Fortunately John Bigman Jones had been born and bred on Mars, where the gravity was only two fifths normal anyway, so it wasn't too bad. Right now he weighed twenty pounds. On Mars he would have weighed fifty, and on the Earth one hundred and twenty.

He got to the sentry, who had been watching him with amused eyes. The sentry was dressed in the uniform of the Lunar National Guard, and he was used to the gravity.

John Bigman Jones said, "Hey. Don't stand there so gloomylike. I brought you a beer. Have it on me."

The sentry looked surprised, then said regretfully, "I can't. Not when I'm on duty, you know."

"Oh well. I can handle it myself, I guess. I'm John Bigman Jones. Call me Bigman." He only came up to the sentry's chin and the sentry wasn't particularly tall, but Bigman held out his hand as though he were reaching down with it.

"I'm Bert Wilson. You from Mars?" The sentry looked at Bigman's scarlet and vermilion hip boots. Nobody but a Martian farm boy would let himself be caught dead in space with them.

Bigman looked down at them proudly. "You bet. I'm stuck here for about a week. Great space, what a rock the Moon is. Don't any of you guys ever go out on the surface?"

"Sometimes. When we have to. There isn't much to see there."

"I sure wish I could go. I hate being cooped up."

"There's a surface lock back there."

Bigman followed the thumb that had been jerked back across the sergeant's shoulder. The corridor (rather poorly lit at this distance from Luna City) narrowed into a recess in the wall.

Bigman said, "I don't have a suit."

"You couldn't go out even if you had one. No one's allowed out without a special pass for a while."

"How come?"

Wilson yawned. "They've got a ship out there that's getting set to go," he looked at his watch, "in about twelve minutes. Maybe the heat will be off after it's gone. I don't know the story on it."

The sentry rocked on the balls of his feet and watched the last of the beer drain down Bigman's throat. He said, "Say, did you get the beer at Patsy's Port Bar? Is it crowded?"

"It's empty. Listen, tell you what. It'll take you fifteen seconds to get in there and have one. I've got nothing to do. I'll stay right here and make sure nothing happens while you're gone."

Wilson looked longingly in the direction of the Port Bar. "I better not."

"It's up to you."

Neither one of them, apparently, was conscious of the figure that drifted past behind them along the corridor and into the recess where the space-lock's huge door barred the way to the surface.

Wilson's feet took him a few steps toward the Bar, as though they were dragging the rest of him. Then he said, "Nah! I better not."

*Ten minutes to zero time.*

It had been Lucky Starr's idea. He had been in Conway's home office the day the news arrived that the T.S.S. *Waltham Zachary* had been gutted by pirates, its cargo gone, its officers frozen corpses in space and most of the men captives. The ship itself had put up a pitifully futile fight and had been too damaged to be worth the pirates' salvage. They had taken everything movable though, the instruments, of course, and even the motors.

Lucky said, "It's the asteroid belt that's the enemy. One hundred thousand rocks."

"More than that." Conway spat out his cigarette. "But what can we do? Ever since the Terrestrial Empire has been a going concern, the asteroids have been more than we could handle. A dozen times we've gone in there to clean out nests of them, and each time we've left enough to breed the troubles again. Twenty-five years ago, when—"

The white-haired scientist stopped short. Twenty-five years ago Lucky's parents had been killed in space and he himself, a little boy, had been cast adrift.

Lucky's calm brown eyes showed no emotion. He said, "The trouble is we don't even know where all the asteroids are."

"Naturally not. It would take a hundred ships a hundred years to get the necessary information for the sizable asteroids. And even then the pull of Jupiter would be forever changing asteroidal orbits here and there."

"We might still try. If we sent out one ship, the pirates might not know it was an impossible job and fear the consequences of a real mapping. If the word got out that we had started a mapping survey, the ship would be attacked."

"And then what?"

"Suppose we sent out an automatic ship, completely equipped, but with no human personnel."

"It would be an expensive thing to do."

"It might be worth it. Suppose we equipped it with lifeboats automatically designed to leave the ship when its instruments recorded the energy pattern of an approaching hyperatomic motor. What do you suppose the pirates would do?"

"Shoot the lifeboats into metal drift, board the ship, and take it to their base."

"Or one of their bases. Right. And if they see the lifeboats try to get away, they won't be surprised at finding no crew aboard. After all, it would be an unarmed survey ship. You wouldn't expect the crew to attempt resistance."

"Well, what are you getting at?"

"Suppose further that the ship is wired to explode once its temperature is raised to more than twenty degrees absolute, as it certainly would if it were brought into an asteroid hangar."

"You're proposing a booby trap, then?"

"A gigantic one. It would blow an asteroid apart. It might destroy dozens of pirate ships. Furthermore, the observatories at Ceres, Vesta, Juno, or Pallas might pick up the flash. Then, if we could locate surviving pirates, we might get information that would be very useful indeed."

"I see."

And so they started work on the *Atlas*.

The shadowy figure in the recess leading to the Moon's surface worked with sure quickness. The sealed controls of the air-lock gave under the needle beam of a micro-heatgun. The shielding metal disc swung open. Busy, black-gloved fingers flew for a moment. Then the disc was replaced and fused tightly back by a wider and cooler beam from the same heatgun.

The cave door of the lock yawned. The alarm that rang routinely whenever it did so was silent this time, its circuits behind the tampered disc disarranged. The figure entered the lock and the door closed behind him. Before he opened the surface door that faced out into the vacuum, he unrolled the pliant plastic he carried under his arm. He scrambled into it, the material covering him wholly and clinging to him, broken only by a strip of clear silicone plastic across his eyes. A small cylinder of liquid oxygen was clamped to a short hose that led to the headpiece and was hooked on to the belt. It was a semi-space-suit, designed for the quick trip across an airless surface, not guaranteed to be serviceable for stretches of more than half an hour.

Bert Wilson, startled, swiveled his head. "Did you hear that?"

Bigman gaped at the sentry. "I didn't hear anything."

"I could swear it was a lock door closing. There isn't any alarm, though."

"Is there supposed to be?"

"Sure. You've got to know when one door is open. It's a bell where there's air and a light where there isn't. Otherwise someone is liable to open the other door and blow all the air out of a ship or corridor."

"All right. If there's no alarm, there's nothing to worry about."

"I'm not so sure." With flat leaps, each one covering twenty feet in the Moon's baby gravity, the sentry passed up the corridor to the air-lock recess. He stopped at a wall panel on the way and activated three separate banks of ceiling Floressoes, turning the area into a noonday of light.

Bigman followed, leaping clumsily and in perpetual danger of overbalancing into a slow nose landing.

Wilson had his blaster out. He inspected the door, then turned to look up the corridor again. "Are you sure you didn't hear anything?"

"Nothing," said Bigman. "Of course, I wasn't listening."

*Five minutes to zero time.*

Pumice kicked up as the space-suited figure moved slow-motion toward the *Atlas*. The space-ship glittered in the Earthlight, but on the Moon's airless surface the light did not carry even an inch into the shadow of the ridge that hemmed in the port.

In three long leaps the figure moved across the lighted portion and into the pitchy shadow of the ship itself.

He moved up the ladder hand over hand, flinging himself into an upward drift that carried him ten rungs at a time. He came to the ship's air-lock. A moment at the controls and it yawned open, then closed.

The *Atlas* had a passenger. One passenger!

The sentry stood before the corridor air-lock and considered its appearance dubiously.

Bigman was rattling on. He said, "I been here nearly a week. I'm supposed to follow my side-kick around and make sure he doesn't get into trouble. How's that for a space wrangler like me. I haven't had a chance to get away—"

The anguished sentry said, "Give it a rest, friend. Look, you're a nice kid and all that, but let's have it some other time."

For a moment he stared at the control seal. "That's funny," he said.

Bigman was swelling ominously. His little face had reddened. He seized the sentry by the elbow and swung him about, almost overbalancing himself as he did so.

"Hey, bud, who're you calling a kid?"

"Look, go away!"

"Just a minute. Let's get something straight. Don't think I let myself get pushed around because I'm not as tall as the next fellow. Put 'em up. Go ahead. Get your fists up or I'll splatter your nose all over your face."

He was sparring and slipping about.

Wilson looked at him with astonishment. "What's got into you? Stop being foolish."

"Scared?"

"I can't fight on duty. Besides, I didn't mean to hurt your feelings. I've just got a job to do and I haven't got any time for you."

Bigman lowered his fists. "Hey, I guess the ship's taking off."

There was no sound, of course, since sound would not travel through a vacuum, but the ground under their feet vibrated softly in response to the hammer blows of a rocket exhaust lifting a ship off a planet.

"That's it, all right." Wilson's forehead creased. "Guess there's no use making a report. It's too late anyway." He had forgotten about the control seal.

*Zero time!*

The ceramic-lined exhaust pit yawned under the *Atlas* and the main rockets blasted their fury into it. Slowly and majestically the ship lifted and moved upward ponderously. Its speed increased. It pierced the black sky, shrinking until it was only a star among stars, and then it was gone.

Dr. Henree looked at his watch for the fifth time and said. "Well, it's gone. It must be gone now." He pointed with the stem of his pipe to the dial.

Conway said, "Let's check with the port authorities."

Five seconds later they were looking at the empty space-port on the visiscreen. The exhaust pit was still open. Even in the near-ultimate frigidity of the Moon's dark side it was still steaming.

Conway shook his head. "It was a beautiful ship."

"Still is."

"I think of it in the past. In a few days it will be a rain of molten metal. It's a doomed ship."

"Let's hope that there's a pirate base somewhere that's also doomed."

Henree nodded somberly.

They both turned as the door opened. It was only Bigman.

He broke into a grin. "Oh, boy, it was sure nice coming in to Luna City. You could feel the pounds going back on with each step you took." He stamped his feet and hopped two or three times. "See," he said, "you try that out where I was and you hit the ceiling and look like one big fool."

Conway frowned. "Where's Lucky?"

Bigman said, "I know where he is. I know where he is every minute. Say, the *Atlas* has just taken off."

"I know that," said Conway. "And where is Lucky?"

"On the *Atlas,* of course. Where do you think he'd be?"

# 2

## Vermin of Space

Dr. Henree dropped his pipe and it bounced on the linolite flooring. He paid it no attention.

"What!"

Conway reddened and his face stood out, plumply pink, against his snowy hair. "Is this a joke?"

"No. He got on five minutes before it blasted. I talked to the sentry, guy called Wilson, and kept him from interfering. I had to pick a fight with the fellow and I would have given him the old bingo-bango," he demonstrated the one-two punch with quick, hard blows at the atmosphere, "but he backed off."

"You let him? You didn't warn us?"

"How could I? I've got to do what Lucky says. He said he had to get on at the last minute and without anyone knowing, or you and Dr. Henree would have stopped him."

Conway groaned. "He did it. By space, Gus, I should have known better than to trust that pint-sized Martian. Bigman, you fool! You know that ship's a booby trap."

"Sure. Lucky knows it too. He says not to send out ships after him or things will be ruined."

"They will, will they? There'll be men after him within the hour just the same."

Henree clutched his friend's sleeve. "Maybe not, Hector. We don't know what he's planning to do, but we can trust him to scramble out safely whatever it is. Let's not interfere."

Conway fell back, trembling with anger and anxiety.

Bigman said, "He says we're to meet him on Ceres, and also, Dr. Conway, he says you're to control your temper."

"You—" began Conway, and Bigman left the room in a hurry.


The orbit of Mars lay behind and the sun was a shrunken thing.

Lucky Starr loved the silence of space. Since he had graduated and joined the Council of Science, space had been his home, rather than any planetary surface. And the *Atlas* was a comfortable ship. It had been provisioned for a full crew with only so much omitted as might be explained by consumption before reaching the asteroids. In every way the *Atlas* was intended to look as though, until the moment of the pirates' appearance, it had been fully manned.

So Lucky ate Syntho-steak from the yeast beds of Venus, Martian pastry, and boneless chicken from Earth.

I'll get fat, he thought, and watched the skies.

He was close enough to make out the larger

asteroids. There was Ceres, the largest of all, nearly five hundred miles in diameter. Vesta was on the other side of the sun, but Juno and Pallas were in sight.

If he were to use the ship's telescope, he would have found more, thousands more, maybe tens of thousands. There was no end to them.

Once it had been thought that there had been a planet between Mars and Jupiter and that geologic ages earlier it had exploded into fragments, but that wasn't so. It was Jupiter that was the villain. Its giant gravitational influence had disrupted space for hundreds of millions of miles about it in the eons when the Solar System was being formed. The cosmic gravel between itself and Mars could never coalesce into a single planet with Jupiter pulling and pulling. Instead it coalesced into myriads of little worlds.

There were the four largest, each a hundred or more miles in diameter. There were fifteen hundred more that were ten and a hundred miles in diameter. After that there were thousands (no one knew exactly how many) that were between one and ten miles in diameter and tens of thousands that were less than a mile in diameter but still as large or larger than the Great Pyramid.

They were so plentiful that astronomers called them "the vermin of space."

The asteroids were scattered over the entire region between Mars and Jupiter, each whirling in its own orbit. No other planetary system known to man in all the Galaxy had such an asteroid belt.

In a sense it was good. The asteroids had formed steppingstones out toward the major planets. In a sense it was bad. Any criminal who could escape to the asteroids was safe from capture by all but the most improbable chance. No police force could search every one of those flying mountains.

The smaller asteroids were no man's land. There were well-manned astronomical observatories on the largest, notably on Ceres. There were beryllium mines on Pallas, while Vesta and Juno were important fueling stations. But that still left fifty thousand sizable asteroids over which the Terrestrial Empire had no control whatever. A few were large enough to harbor fleets. Some were too small for more than a single speed-cruiser with additional space, perhaps, for a six-month supply of fuel, food, and water.

And it was impossible to map them. Even in the ancient, preatomic times, before space travel, when only fifteen hundred or so were known, and those the largest, mapping had been impossible. Their orbits had been carefully calculated via telescopic observation and still asteroids were forever being "lost," then "found" again.

Lucky snapped out of his reverie. The sensitive Ergometer was picking up pulsations from the outer reaches. He was at the control board in a step.

The steady energy outpourings of the sun, whether direct or by way of the relatively tiny reflected dribbles from the planets, were canceled out on the meter. What was coming in now were the characteristically intermittent energy pulses of a hyperatomic motor.

Lucky threw in the Ergograph connection and the energy pattern traced itself out in a series of lines. He followed the graphed paper as it emerged and his jaw muscles hardened.

There had always been a chance that the *Atlas* might meet an ordinary trading ship or passenger liner, but the energy pattern was none of that. The approaching ship had motors of advanced design, and different from any of the Terrestrial fleet.

Five minutes passed before he had enough spread of measurement to be able to calculate the distance and direction of the energy source.

He adjusted the visiplate for telescopic viewing and the star field speckled enormously. Carefully he searched among the infinitely silent, infinitely distant, infinitely motionless stars until a flicker of movement caught his eyes and the Ergometer's reading dials lined up at multiple zero.

It was a pirate. No doubt! He could make out its outlines by the half that glittered in the sun and by the port lights in the shaded half. It was a thin, graceful vessel, having the look of speed and maneuverability. It had an alien look about it, too.

Sirian design, thought Lucky.

He watched the ship grow slowly larger on the screen. Was it such a ship that his father and mother watched on the last day of their lives?

He scarcely remembered his father and mother, but he had seen pictures of them and had heard endless stories about Lawrence and Barbara Starr from Henree and Conway. They had been inseparable, the tall, grave Gus Henree, the choleric, persevering Hector Conway, and the quick, laughing Larry Starr. They had gone to school together, graduated simultaneously,

entered the Council as one and done all their as-
signments as a team.

And then Lawrence Starr had been promoted and
assigned to a tour of duty on Venus. He, his wife, and
his four-year-old son were Venus-bound when the
pirate ship attacked.

For years Lucky had unhappily imagined what that
last hour upon the dying ship must have been like.
First, the crippling of the main power drives at the
stern of the ship while pirate and victim were still
apart. Then the blasting of the air-locks and the
boarding. The crew and passengers scrambling into
space-suits against the loss of air when the air-locks
caved in. The crew armed and waiting. The passengers
huddling in the interior rooms without much hope.
Women weeping. Children screaming.

His father wasn't among the hiders. His father was a
Council member. He had been armed and fighting.
Lucky was sure of that. He had one memory, a short
one that had been burned into his mind. His father, a
tall, strong man, was standing with blaster raised and
face set in what must have been one of the few
moments of cold rage in his life, as the door of the
control room crashed inward in a cloud of black
smoke. And his mother, face wet and smudged but
clearly seen through the space-suit face-plate, was
forcing him into a small lifeboat.

"Don't cry, David, it will be all right."

Those were the only words he remembered ever
having heard his mother say. Then there was thunder
behind him and he was pressed back against a wall.

They found him in the lifeboat two days later,

when they followed its coldly automatic radio calls for help.

The government had launched a tremendous campaign against the asteroid pirates immediately afterward and the Council had lent that drive every last ounce of their own effort. For the pirates it turned out that to attack and kill key men of the Council of Science was bad business. Such asteroid hideouts as were located were blasted into dust, and the pirate menace was reduced to the merest flicker for twenty years.

But often Lucky wondered if they had ever located the particular pirate ship that had carried the men who had killed his parents. There was no way of telling.

And now the menace had revived in a less spectacular but far more dangerous fashion. Piracy wasn't a matter of individual jabs any longer. It bore the appearance of an organized attack on Terrestrial commerce. There was more to it. From the nature of the warfare carried on Lucky felt certain that one mind, one strategic direction, lay behind it. That one mind, he knew, he would have to find.

He lifted his eyes to the Ergometer once more. The energy recordings were strong now. The other vessel was well within the distance at which space courtesy required routine messages of mutual identification. For that matter, it was well within the distance at which a pirate might have made its initial hostile move.

The floor shuddered under Lucky. It wasn't a blaster bolt from the other ship, but rather the recoil of a departing lifeboat. The energy pulses had become strong enough to activate their automatic controls.

Another shudder. And another. Five altogether.

He watched the oncoming ship closely. Often pirates shot up such lifeboats, partly out of the perverted fun of it and partly to prevent escapees from describing the vessel, assuming they had not done so already through the sub-ether.

This time, however, the ship ignored the lifeboats altogether. It approached within locking range. Its magnetic grapples shot out, clamped on the *Atlas*'s hull, and the two vessels were suddenly welded together, their motions through space well matched.

Lucky waited.

He heard the air-lock open, then shut. He heard the clang of feet and the sound of helmets being unclipped, then the sound of voices.

He didn't move.

A figure appeared in the door. Helmet and gauntlets had been removed, but the rest of the man was still swathed in ice-coated space-suit. Space-suits had a habit of doing that when one entered from the near-absolute zero of space into the warm moist air of the interior of a ship. The ice was beginning to melt.

The pirate caught sight of Lucky only when he was two full steps into the control room. He stopped, his face frozen in an almost comical expression of surprise. Lucky had time to note the sparse black hair, the long nose, and the dead white scar that ran from nostril to canine tooth splitting the upper lip into two unequal parts.

Lucky bore the pirate's astonished scrutiny calmly. He had no fear of recognition. Councilmen on active duty always worked without publicity with the very thought that a too-well-known face would diminish their usefulness. His own father's face had appeared over the sub-ether only after his death. With fleeting bitterness Lucky thought that perhaps better publicity during life might have prevented the pirate attack. But that was silly, he knew. By the time the pirates had seen Lawrence Starr the attack had proceeded too far to be stopped.

Lucky said, "I've got a blaster. I'll use it only if you reach for yours. Don't move."

The pirate had opened his mouth. He closed it again.

Lucky said, "If you want to call the rest, go ahead."

The pirate stared suspiciously, then, eyes firmly on Lucky's blaster, yelled, "Blinking space, there's a ripper with a gat here."

There was laughter at that, and a voice shouted, "Quiet!"

Another man stepped into the room. "Step aside, Dingo," he said.

His space-suit was off entirely and he was an incongruous sight aboard ship. His clothing might have come out of the most fashionable tailor shop in International City, and would have suited better a dinner party back on Earth. His shirt had a silken look you got only out of the best plastex. Its iridescence was subtle rather than garish, and his tight-ankled breeches blended in so well that, but for the ornamented belt, it would have seemed one garment. He wore a wristband that matched his belt and a fluffy, sky-blue neck sash. His crisp brown hair was curly and looked as though it received frequent attention.

He was half a head shorter than Lucky, but from the way he carried himself the young Councilman could see that any assumption of softness he might make on the basis of the man's dude costume would be quite wrong.

The newcomer said pleasantly, "Anton is my name. Would you put down your gun?"

Lucky said, "And be shot?"

"You may be shot eventually, but not at the moment. I would like to question you first."

Lucky held fast.

Anton said, "I keep my word." A tiny flush appeared on his cheekbones. "It is my only virtue as men count virtue, but I hold fast to it."

Lucky put down his blaster and Anton picked it up. He handed it to the other pirate.

"Put it away, Dingo, and get out of here." He turned to Lucky. "The other passengers got away in the lifeboats? Right?"

Lucky said, "That's an obvious trap, Anton—"

"Captain Anton, *please.*" He smiled, but his nostrils flared.

"Well, then, it's a trap, Captain Anton. It was obvious that you knew there were no passengers or crew on this ship. You knew it long before you boarded."

"Indeed? How do you make that out?"

"You approached the ship without signaling and without a warning shot. You made no particular speed. You ignored the lifeboats when they shot out. Your men entered the ship carelessly, as though they expected no resistance. The man who first found me entered this room with his blaster well holstered. The conclusion follows."

"Very good. And what are you doing on a ship without crew or passengers?"

Lucky said grimly, "I came to see you, Captain Anton."

# 3

## Duel in Word

Anton's expression did not change. "And now you see me."

"But not privately, Captain." Lucky's lips thinned and closed with great deliberation.

Anton looked quickly about. A dozen of his men in every stage of space-suit undress had crowded into the room, watching and listening with gaping interest.

He reddened slightly. His voice rose. "Get on your business, scum. I want a complete report on this ship. And keep your weapons ready. There may be more men on board and if anyone else gets caught as Dingo did, he'll be tossed out an air-lock."

There was slow, shuffling motion outward.

Anton's voice was a sudden scream. "Quickly! Quickly!" One snaking gesture, and a blaster was in his hand. "I'll count three and shoot. One . . . two . . ."

They were gone.

He faced Lucky again. His eyes glittered and his

breath came and went quickly through pinched white nostrils.

"Discipline is a great thing," he breathed. "They must fear me. They must fear me more than they fear capture by the Terrestrial Navy. Then a ship is one mind and one arm."

Yes, thought Lucky, one mind and one arm, but whose? Yours?

Anton's smile had returned, boyish, friendly, and open. "Now tell me what you want."

Lucky jerked a thumb toward the other's blaster, still drawn and ready. He matched the other's smile. "Do you intend shooting? If so, get it over with."

Anton was shaken. "Space! You're a cool one. I'll shoot when I please. I like it this way. What's your name?" The blaster held on its line with deadly steadiness.

"Williams, Captain."

"You're a tall man, Williams. You look strong. And yet here I sit and with just a pressure of my thumb you're dead. I think it's very instructive. Two men and one blaster is the whole secret of power. Did you ever think of power, Williams?"

"Sometimes."

"It's the only meaning to life, don't you think?"

"Maybe."

"I see you're anxious to do business. Let's begin. Why are you here?"

"I've heard of pirates."

"We're the men of the asteroids, Williams. No other name."

"That suits me. I've come to join the men of the asteroids."

"You flatter us, but my thumb is still on the blaster contact. Why do you want to join?"

"Life is closed on Earth, Captain. A man like myself could settle down to be an accountant or an engineer. I might even run a factory or sit behind a desk and vote at stockholders' meetings. It doesn't matter. Whatever it is, it would be routine. I would know my life from beginning to end. There would be no adventure, no uncertainty."

"You're a philosopher, Williams. Go on."

"There are the colonies, but I'm not attracted by a life as a farm boy on Mars on as a vat tender on Venus. What does attract me is the life on the asteroids. You live hard and dangerously. A man can rise to power as you have. As you say, power gives meaning to life."

"So you stow away on an empty ship?"

"I didn't know it was empty. I had to stow away somewhere. Legitimate space passage comes high and passports to the asteroids aren't being handed out these days. I knew this ship was part of a mapping expedition. The word had got around. It was headed for the asteroids. So I waited till just before it blasted off. That's when everybody would be busy getting ready for takeoff and yet the air-locks would still be open. I had a pal take a sentry out of circulation.

"I figured we'd stop at Ceres. It would be bound to be Prime Base for any asteroid expedition. Once there, it seemed to me I could get off without trouble. The crew would be astronomers and mathematicians. Snatch off their glasses and they'd be blind. Point a blaster at them and they'd die of fright. Once on

Ceres I'd contact the pi—— The men of the asteroids, somehow. Simple."

"Only you got a surprise when you boarded ship? Is that it?" asked Anton.

"I'll say. No one aboard and before I could get it straight in my mind that there *wasn't* anyone aboard, it blasted off."

"What's it all about, Williams? How do you figure it?"

"I don't. It beats me."

"Well, let's see if we can find out. You and I together." He gestured with his blaster and said sharply, "Come on."

The pirate chief led the way out of the control room into the long central corridor of the ship. A group of men came out of a door up ahead. They rumbled short comments at one another and stilled into silence when they caught Anton's eyes.

Anton said, "Come here."

They approached. One wiped a grizzled mustache with the back of his hand and said, "No one else on board this ship, Captain."

"All right. What do you think of the ship?"

There were four of them. The number increased as more men joined the group.

Anton's voice grew edgy. "What do any of you think of the ship?"

Dingo pushed his way forward. He had got rid of his space-suit and Lucky could see him as a man. It was not altogether a pleasant sight. He was broad and heavy and his arms were slightly bowed as they hung loosely from bulging shoulders. There were tufts of dark hair on the back of his fingers and the scar on his upper lip twitched. His eyes glared at Lucky.

He said, "I don't like it."

"You don't like the ship?" Anton asked sharply.

Dingo hesitated. He straightened his arms, threw back his shoulders. "It stinks."

"Why? Why do you say that?"

"I could take it apart with a can opener. Ask the rest and see if they don't agree with me. This crate is put together with toothpicks. It wouldn't hold together for three months."

There were murmurs of agreement. The man with the gray mustache said, "Beg your pardon, Captain, but the wiring is taped in place. It's a two-bit job. The insulation is almost burnt through already."

"All the welding was done in a real hurry," said another. "The seams stand out like that." He held out a thick and dirty thumb.

"What about repairs?" asked Anton.

Dingo said, "It would take a year and a Sunday. It isn't worth it. Anyway, we couldn't do it here. We'd have to take it to one of the rocks."

Anton turned to Lucky, explaining suavely, "We always refer to the asteroids as 'rocks,' you understand."

Lucky nodded.

Anton said, "Apparently my men feel that they wouldn't care to ride this ship. Why do you suppose the Earth government would sent out an empty ship and such a jerry-built job to boot?"

"It keeps getting more and more confusing," said Lucky.

"Let's complete our investigation, then."

Anton walked first. Lucky followed closely. The men tagged behind silently. The back of Lucky's neck prickled. Anton's back was straight and fearless, as though he expected no attack from Lucky. He might well feel so. Ten armed men were on Lucky's heels.

They glanced through the small rooms, each designed for utmost economy in space. There was the computation room, the small observatory, the photographic laboratory, the galley and the bunk rooms.

They slipped down to the lower level through a narrow curving tube within which the pseudo-grav field was neutralized so that either direction could be "up" or "down" at will. Lucky was motioned down first, Anton following so closely that Lucky barely had time to scramble out of the way (his legs buckling slightly with the sudden access of weight) before the pirate chief was upon him. Hard, heavy space-boots missed his face by inches.

Lucky regained his balance and whirled angrily, but Anton was standing there smiling pleasantly, his blaster lined up straight and true at Lucky's heart.

"A thousand apologies," he said. "Fortunately you are quite agile."

"Yes," muttered Lucky.

On the lower level were the engine room and the power plant; the empty berths where the lifeboats had been. There were the fuel stores, the food and water stores, the air fresheners, and the atomic shielding.

Anton murmured, "Well, what do you think of it all? Shoddy, perhaps, but I see nothing out of order."

"It's hard to tell like this," said Lucky.

"But you must have lived on this ship for days."

"Sure, but I didn't spend time looking it over. I just waited for it to get somewhere."

"I see. Well, back to upper level."

Lucky was first "down" the travel tube again. This time he landed lightly and sprang six feet to one side with the grace of a cat.

Seconds passed before Anton popped out of the tube. "Jumpy?" he asked.

Lucky flushed.

One by one the pirates appeared. Anton did not wait for all of them, but started down the corridor again.

"You know," he said, "you'd think we'd been all over this ship. Most people would say so. Wouldn't you say so?"

"No," said Lucky calmly, "I wouldn't. We haven't been in the washroom."

Anton scowled and for more than just a moment the pleasantness was gone from his face, and only a tight, white anger flashed in its place.

Then it passed. He adjusted a stray lock of hair on his head, then regarded the back of his hand with interest. "Well, let's look there."

Several of the men whistled and the rest exclaimed in a variety of ways when the appropriate door clicked open.

"Very nice," murmured Anton. "Very nice. Luxurious, I would say."

It was! There was no question of that. There were separate stall showers, three of them, with their plumbing arranged for sudsing water (luke-warm) and rinsing water (hot or cold). There were also half a dozen washbowls in ivory-chrome, with shampoo stands, hair driers and needle-jet skin stimulators. Nothing that was necessary was missing.

"There's certainly nothing shoddy about this," said Anton. "It's like a show on the sub-etherics, eh, Williams? What do you make of this?"

"I'm confused."

Anton's smile vanished like the fleeting flash of a speeding space-ship across a visiplate. "I'm not. Dingo, come in here."

The pirate chief said to Lucky, "It's a simple problem, you. We have a ship here with no one aboard, thrown together in the cheapest possible way, as though it were done in a hurry, but with a washroom that is the last word. Why? I think it's just in order to have as many pipes as possible *in* the washroom. And why that? So that we'd never suspect that one or two of them were dummies . . . Dingo, which pipe is it?"

Dingo kicked one.

"Well, don't kick it, you misbegotten fool. Take it apart."

Dingo did so, a micro-heatgun flashing briefly. He yanked out wires.

"What's that, Williams?" demanded Anton.

"Wires," said Lucky briefly.

"I know that, you lump." He was suddenly furious. "What else? I'll tell *you* what else. Those wires are set to explode every ounce of the atomite on board ship as soon as we take the ship back to base."

Lucky jumped. "How can you tell that?"

"You're surprised? You didn't know this was one

big trap? You didn't know we were supposed to take this back to base for repairs? You didn't know we were supposed to explode ourselves and the base, too, into hot dust? Why, you're here as the bait to make sure we were properly fooled. Only I'm not a fool!"

His men were crowding close. Dingo licked his lips.

With a snap Anton brought up his blaster and there was no mercy, no dream of mercy, in his eyes.

"Wait! Great Galaxy, wait! I know nothing about this. You have no right to shoot me without cause." He tensed for a jump, one last fight before death.

"No right!" Anton, eyes glaring, lowered his blaster suddenly. "How dare you say no right. I have all rights on this ship."

"You can't kill a good man. The men of the asteroids need good men. Don't throw one away for nothing."

A sudden, unexpected murmur came from some of the pirates.

A voice said, "He's got guts, Cap'n. Maybe we could use—"

It died away as Anton turned.

He turned back. "What makes you a good man, Williams? Answer that and I'll consider."

"I'll hold my own against anyone here. Bare fists or any weapon."

"So?" Anton's teeth bared themselves. "You hear that, men?"

There was an affirmative roar.

"It's your challenge, Williams. Any weapon. Good! Come out of this alive and you won't be shot. You'll be considered for membership in my crew."

"I have your word, Captain?"

"You have my word, and I never break my word. The crew hears me. *If* you come out of this alive."

"Whom do I fight?" demanded Lucky.

"Dingo here. A good man. Anyone who can beat him is a *very* good man."

Lucky measured the huge lump of gristle and sinew standing before him, its little eyes glittering with anticipation, and glumly agreed with the captain.

But he said firmly, "What weapons? Or is it bare fists?"

"Weapons! Push-tubes, to be exact. Push-tubes in open space."

For a moment Lucky found it difficult to maintain an appropriate stolidity.

Anton smiled. "Are you afraid it won't be a proper test for you? Don't be. Dingo is the best man with a push-gun in our entire fleet."

Lucky's heart plummeted. A push-gun duel required an expert. Notoriously so! Played as he had played it in college days, it was a sport. Fought by professionals, it was deadly!

And he was no professional!

# 4

## Duel in Deed

Pirates crowded the outer skin of the *Atlas* and of their own Sirian-designed ship. Some were standing, held by the magnetic field of their boots. Others had cast themselves loose for better viewing, maintaining their place by means of a short magnetic cable attached to the ship's hull.

Fifty miles apart two metal-foil goal posts had been set. Not more than three feet square in their collapsed state aboard ship, they opened into a hundred feet either way of thin-beaten beryl-magnesium sheets. Undimmed and undamaged in the great emptiness of space, they were set spinning, and the flickering reflections of the sun on their gleaming surfaces sent beams that were visible for miles.

"You know the rules." Anton's voice was loud in Lucky's ears, and presumably in Dingo's ears as well.

Lucky could make out the other's space-suited shape as a sunlit speck half a mile away. The lifeboat that had brought them here was racing away now, back toward the pirate ship.

"You know the rules," said Anton's voice. "The

one who gets pushed back to his own goal post is the loser. If neither gets pushed back, the one whose push-gun expires first is the loser. No time limit. No off-side. You have five minutes to get set. The push-gun can't be used till the word is given."

No off-side, thought Lucky. That was the giveaway. Push duels as a legal sport could not take place more than a hundred miles from an asteroid at least fifty miles in diameter. This would place a definite, though small, gravitational pull on the players. It would not be enough to affect mobility. It would be enough, however, to rescue a contestant who found himself miles out in space with an expired push-gun. Even if not picked up by the rescue boat he had only to remain quiet and in a matter of hours or, at most, one or two days, he would drift back to the asteroid's surface.

Here, on the other hand, there was no sizable asteroid within hundreds of thousands of miles. A real push would continue indefinitely. It would end, as likely as not, in the sun, long after the unlucky contestant had smothered to death when his oxygen gave out. Under such conditions it was usually understood that, when one contestant or another passed outside certain set limits, time was called until their return.

Saying "no off-side" was saying "to the death."

Anton's voice came clear and sharp across the miles of space between himself and the radio receiver in Lucky's helmet. He said, "Two minutes to go. Adjust body signals."

Lucky brought his hand up and closed the switch set into his chest. The colored metal foil which had earlier been magnet-set into his helmet was spinning.

It was a miniature goal post. Dingo's figure, a moment before merely a dim dot, now sprang into flickering ruddy life. His own signal, Lucky knew, was a flashing green. And the goal posts were pure white.

Even now a fraction of Lucky's mind was far away. He had tried to make one objection at the very beginning. He had said, "Look, this all suits me, you understand. But while we're fooling around, a government patrol ship might——"

Anton barked contemptuously, "Forget it. No patrol ship would have the guts to get this far into the rocks. We've a hundred ships within call, a thousand rocks to hold us if we had to make a getaway. Get into your suit."

A hundred ships! A thousand rocks! If true, the pirates had never yet shown their full hand. What was going on?

"One minute left!" said Anton's voice through space.

Grimly Lucky brought up his two push-guns. They were L-shaped objects connected by springy, gummed fabric tubing to the doughnutlike gas cylinders (containing carbon dioxide liquid under great pressure) that had been adjusted about his waist. In the old days the connecting tubing had been metal mesh. But that, though stronger, had also been more massive and had added to the momentum and inertia of the guns. In push duels rapid aiming and firing was essential. Once a fluorinated silicone had been invented which could remain a flexible gum at space temperatures and yet not become tacky in the direct rays of the sun, the lighter tubing material was universally used.

"Fire when ready!" cried Anton.

One of Dingo's push-guns triggered for an instant. The liquid carbon dioxide of his gas cylinder bubbled into violent gas and spurted out through the push-gun's needlelike orifice. The gas froze into a line of tiny crystals within six inches of its point of emersion. Even in the half second allowed for release a line of crystals, miles long, had been formed. As they pushed out one way, Dingo was pushed in the other. It was a spaceship and its rocket blast in miniature.

Three times the "crystal line" flashed and faded in the distance. It pointed into space directly away from Lucky, and each time Dingo gained speed toward Lucky. The actual state of affairs was deceptive. The only change visible to the eye was the slow brightening of Dingo's suit signal, but Lucky knew that the distance between them was closing with hurtling velocity.

What Lucky did not know was the proper strategy to expect; the appropriate defense. He waited to let the other's offensive moves unfold.

Dingo was large enough now to see as a humanoid shape with head and four limbs. He was passing to one side, and making no move to adjust his aim. He seemed content to bear far to Lucky's left.

Lucky still waited. The chorus of confused cries that rang in his helmet had died down. They came from the open transmitters of the audience. Though these were too far away to see the contestants, they could still follow the passage of the body signals and the flashes of the carbon dioxide streams. They were expecting something, Lucky thought.

It came suddenly.

A blast of carbon dioxide, then another appeared to Dingo's right, and his line of flight veered toward the young Councilman's position. Lucky brought his push-gun up, ready to flash downward and avoid close quarters. The safest strategy, he thought, was to do just that, and to move as slowly and as little as possible otherwise, in order to conserve carbon dioxide.

But Dingo's flight did not continue toward Lucky. He fired straight ahead of himself, a long streak, and began to recede. Lucky watched him, and only too late the streak of light met his eyes.

The line of carbon dioxide that Dingo had last fired traveled forward, yes, but he had been moving leftward at the time and so it did likewise. The two motions together moved it directly toward Lucky and it struck his left shoulder bull's-eye.

To Lucky it felt like a sharp blow pounding him. The crystals were tiny, but they extended for miles and they were traveling at miles per second. They all hit his suit in the space of what seemed a fraction of an eyelid's flicker. Lucky's suit trembled and the roar of the audience was in his ear.

"You got him, Dingo!"

"What a blast!"

"Straight toward goal post. Look at him!"

"It was beautiful. Beautiful!"

"Look at the joker spin!"

Underneath that there were murmurs that seemed, somehow, less exuberant.

Lucky was spinning or, rather, it seemed to his eyes that the heavens and all the stars in it were spinning. Across the face-plate of his helmet the stars

were white streaks, as though they were sparkles of
trillions of carbon dioxide crystals themselves.

He could see nothing but the numerous blurs. For
a moment it was as though the blow had knocked the
power of thinking out of him.

A blow in the midriff and one in the back sent
him, still spinning, further on his hurtling way
through space.

He had to do something or Dingo would make a
football of him from one end of the Solar System to
the other. The first thing was to stop the spin and get
his bearings. He was tumbling diagonally, left shoulder over right hip. He pointed the push-gun in the
direction counter to that twist, and in lightning re-
leases pumped out streams of carbon dioxide.

The stars slowed until their turning was a stately
march that left them sharply defined points. The sky
became the familiar sky of space.

One star flickered and was too bright. Lucky knew
it to be his own goal post. Almost diametrically opposed was the angry red of Dingo's body signal.
Lucky could not fling himself backward beyond the
goal post or the duel would be over and he would
have lost. Beyond the goal post and within a mile of
it was the standard rule for a goal ending. Nor, on
the other hand, could he afford to get closer to his
opponent.

He brought his push-gun straight up over his head,
closed contact, and held it so. He counted a full minute before he released contact, and through all the
sixty seconds he felt the pressure against the top of his
helmet as he accelerated downward.

It was a desperate maneuver, for he threw away a half hour's supply of gas in that one minute.

Dingo, in outrage, yelled hoarsely, "You flumstered coward! You yellow mugger!"

The cries of the audience also rose to a crescendo.

"Look at him run."

"He got past Dingo. Dingo, get him."

"Hey, Williams. Put up a fight."

Lucky saw the crimson blur of his enemy again.

He had to keep on the move. There was nothing else he could do. Dingo was an expert and could hit a one-inch meteorite as it flashed by. He himself, Lucky thought ruefully, would do well to hit Ceres at a mile.

He used his push-guns alternately. To the left, to the right; then quickly, to the right, to the left and to the right again.

It made no difference. It was as though Dingo could foretell his moves, cut across the corners, move in inexorably.

Lucky felt the perspiration beading out upon his forehead, and suddenly he was aware of the silence. He could not remember the exact moment it had come, but it had come like the breaking of a thread. One moment there had been the yells and laughter of the pirates, and the next moment only the dead silence of space where sound could never be heard.

Had he passed beyond range of the ships? Impossible! Suit radios, even the simplest type, would carry thousands of miles in space. He pushed the sensitivity dial on his chest to maximum.

"Captain Anton!"

But it was Dingo's rough voice that answered. "Don't yell. I hear you."

Lucky said, "Call time! There's something wrong with my radio."

Dingo was close enough to be made out as a human figure again. A flashing line of crystals and he was closer. Lucky moved away, but the pirate followed on his heels.

"Nothing wrong," said Dingo. "Just a gimmicked radio. I've been waiting. I've been waiting. I could have knocked you past goal long ago, but I've been waiting for the radio to go. It's just a little transistor I gimmicked before you put on your suit. You can still talk to me, though. It'll still carry a mile or two. Or at least you can talk to me for a little while." He relished the joke and barked his laughter.

Lucky said, "I don't get it."

Dingo's voice turned harshly cruel. "You caught me on the ship with my blaster in its holster. You trapped me there. You made me look like a fool. No one traps me and I don't let anyone make a fool out of me in front of the captain and live very long after that. I'm not goaling you for someone else to finish. I'm finishing you here! Myself!"

Dingo was much closer. Lucky could almost make out the face behind the thick glassite of the face-plate.

Lucky abandoned attempts at bobbing and weaving. That would lead, he decided, to being consistently out-maneuvered. He considered straight flight, pushing outward at increasing velocity as long as his gas held out.

But then afterward? And was he going to be content to die while running away?

He would have to fight back. He aimed the push-gun at Dingo, and Dingo wasn't there when the line of crystals passed through the spot where a moment before he *had* been. He tried again and again, but Dingo was a flitting demon.

And then Lucky felt the hard impact of the other's push-gun blast and he was spinning again. Desperately he tried to come out of the spin and before he could do so, he felt the clanging force of a body's collision with his.

Dingo held his suit in tight embrace.

Helmet to helmet. Face-plate to face-plate. Lucky was staring at the white scar splitting Dingo's upper lip. It spread tightly as Dingo smiled.

"Hello, chum," he said. "Pleased to meet you."

For a moment Dingo floated away, or seemed to, as he loosened the grip of his arms. The pirate's thighs held firm about Lucky's knees, their apelike strength immobilizing him. Lucky's own whipcord muscles wrenched this way and that uselessly.

Dingo's partial retreat had been designed only to free his arms. One lifted high, push-gun held butt-first. It came down directly on the face-plate and Lucky's head snapped back with the sudden, shattering impact. The relentless arm swung up again, while the other curled about Lucky's neck.

"Hold your head still," the pirate snarled. "I'm finishing this."

Lucky knew that to be the literal truth unless he acted quickly. The glassite was strong and tough, but it would hold out only so long against the battering of metal.

He brought up the heel of his gauntleted hand

against Dingo's helmet, straightening his arm and pushing the pirate's head back. Dingo rocked his head to one side, disengaging Lucky's arm. He brought the the butt of his push-gun down a second time.

Lucky dropped both push-guns, let them dangle from their connecting tubes, and with a sure movement snatched at the connecting tubes of Dingo's guns. He threaded them between the fingers of his steel gloves. The muscles of his arms lumped and tightened painfully. His jaws clenched and he felt the blood creep to his temples.

Dingo, his mouth twisted in fierce joyful anticipation, disregarded everything but the upturned face of his victim behind the transparent face-plate, contorted, as he thought, with fear. Once more the butt came down. A small cracking star appeared where the metal had struck.

Then something else gave and the universe seemed to go mad.

First one and, almost immediately afterward, the other of the connecting tubes of Dingo's two push-guns parted and an uncontrollable stream of carbon dioxide raveled out of each broken tube.

The tubes whipped like insane snakes, and Lucky was slammed against his suit first this way, then that, in violent reaction to the mad and uncontrolled acceleration.

Dingo yelled in jolted surprise and his grip loosened.

The two almost separated, but Lucky held on grimly to one of the pirate's ankles.

The carbon dioxide stream slackened and Lucky went up his opponent's leg hand over hand.

They were apparently motionless now. The chance

whippings of the stream had left them even without any perceptible spin. Dingo's push-gun tubes, now dead and flaccid, stretched out in their last position. All seemed still, as still as death.

But that was a delusion. Lucky knew they were traveling at miles per second in whatever direction that last stroke of gas had sent them. They were alone and lost in space, the two of them.

# 5

## The Hermit on the Rock

Lucky was on Dingo's back now and it was his thighs that gripped the other's waist. He spoke softly and grimly. "You can hear me, Dingo, can't you? I don't know where we are or where we're going, but neither do you. So we need each other now, Dingo. Are you ready to make a deal? You can find out where we are because your radio will reach the ships, but you can't get back without carbon dioxide. I have enough for both of us, but I'll need you to guide us back."

"To space with you, you scupper," yelled Dingo. "When I'm done with you, I'll *have* your push-tubes."

"I don't think you will," said Lucky coolly.

"You think you'll let them loose, too. Go ahead! Go ahead, you loshing ripper! What good will that do? The captain will come for me wherever I am while you're floating around with a busted helmet and frozen blood on your face."

"Not exactly, my friend. There is something in your back, you know. Maybe you can't feel it through the metal, but it's there, I assure you."

"A push-gun. So what. It doesn't mean a thing as long as we're held together." But his arms halted their writhing attempt to seize Lucky.

"I'm not a push-gun duelist." Lucky sounded cheerful about it. "But I still know more than you do about push-guns. Push-gun shots are exchanged miles apart. There's no air resistance to slow and mess up the gas stream, but there's internal resistance. There's always some turbulence in the stream. The crystals knock together, slow up. The line of gas widens. If it misses its mark, it finally spreads out in space and vanishes, but if it finally hits, it still kicks like a mule after miles of travel."

"What in space are you talking about? What are you running off about?" The pirate twisted with bull strength, and Lucky grunted as he forced him back.

Lucky said, "Just this. What do you suppose happens when the carbon dioxide hits at two inches, before turbulence has done anything at all to cut down its velocity or to broaden the beam. Don't guess. I'll tell you. It would cut through your suit as though it were a blowtorch, and through your body, too."

"You're nuts! You're talking crazy!"

Dingo swore madly, but of a sudden he was holding his body stiffly motionless.

"Try it, then," said Lucky. "Move! My push-gun is hard against your suit and I'm squeezing the trigger. Try it out."

"You're fouling me," snarled Dingo. "This isn't a clean win."

"I've got a crack in my face plate," said Lucky. "The men will know where the foul is. You have half a minute to make up your mind."

The seconds passed in silence. Lucky caught the motion of Dingo's hand.

He said, "Good-by, Dingo!"

Dingo cried thickly, "Wait! *Wait!* I'm just extending my sending range." Then he called, "Captain Anton . . . Captain Anton . . ."

It took an hour and a half to get back to the ships.


The *Atlas* was moving through space again in the wake of its pirate captor. Its automatic circuits had been shifted to manual controls wherever necessary, and a prize crew of three controlled its power. As before, it had a passenger list of one—Lucky Starr.

Lucky was confined to a cabin and saw the crew only when they brought him his rations. The *Atlas*'s own rations, thought Lucky. Or, at least, such as were left. Most of the food and such equipment that wasn't necessary for the immediate maneuvering of the ship had already been transferred to the pirate vessel.

All three pirates brought him his first meal. They were lean men, browned by the unsoftened rays of the sun of space.

They gave him his tray in silence, inspected the cabin cautiously, stood by while he opened the cans and let their contents warm up, then carried away the remains.

Lucky said, "Sit down, men. You don't have to stand while I eat."

They did not answer. One, the thinnest and lankest of the three, with a nose that had once been broken and was now bent sideways, and an Adam's-apple that jutted sharply outward, looked at the others as though he felt inclined to accept the invitation. He met with no response, however.

The next meal was brought by Broken Nose alone. He put down the tray, went back to the door, which he opened. He looked up and down the corridor, closed the door again, and said, "I'm Martin Maniu."

Lucky smiled. "I'm Bill Williams. The other two don't talk to me, eh?"

"They're Dingo's friends. But I'm not. Maybe you're a government man like the captain thinks, and maybe you're not. I don't know. But as far as I'm concerned, anyone who does what you did to that scupper, Dingo, is all right. He's a wise guy and he plays rough. He got me into a push fight once when I was new. He nearly pushed me into an asteroid. For no reason, either. He claimed it was a mistake, but listen, he doesn't make any mistakes with a pusher. You made quite a few friends, mister, when you dragged back that hyena by the seat of his pants."

"I'm glad of that, anyway."

"But watch out for him. He'll never forget it. Don't be alone with him even twenty years from now. I'm telling you. It isn't just beating him, you see. It's bluffing him with the story about cutting through an inch of metal with the carbon dioxide. Everyone's laughing at him and he's sick about it. Man, I mean sick! It's the best thing that's ever happened. Man, I sure hope the Boss gives you a clean bill."

"The Boss? Captain Anton?"

"No, the Boss. The big fellow. Say, the food you've got on board ship is good. Especially the meat." The pirate smacked his lips loudly. "You get tired of all these yeast mashes, especially when you're in charge of a vat yourself."

Lucky was brushing up the remainder of his meal. "Who *is* this guy?"

"Who?"

"The Boss."

Manui shrugged. "Space! I don't know. You don't think a guy like me would ever meet him. Just someone the fellows talk about. It stands to reason *someone's* boss."

"The organization is pretty complicated."

"Man, you never know till you join. Listen, I was dead broke when I came out here. I didn't know what to do. I thought, well, we'll bang up a few ships and then I'll get mine and it'll be over. You know, it would be better than starving to death like I was doing."

"It wasn't that way?"

"*No.* I've never been on a raiding expedition. Hardly any of us have. Just a few like Dingo. *He* goes out all the time. He likes it, the scupper. Mostly we go out and pick up a few women sometimes." The pirate smiled. "I've got a wife and a kid. You wouldn't believe that now, would you? Sure, we've got a little project of our own. Have our own vats. Once in a while I draw space duty, like now, for instance. It's a soft life. You could do all right, if you join up. A good-looking fellow like you could get a wife in no time and settle down. Or there's plenty of excitement if that's what you want.

"Yes, sir, Bill. I hope the Boss takes you."

Lucky followed him to the door. "Where are we going, by the way? One of the bases?"

"Just to one of the rocks, I guess. Whichever is nearest. You'll stay there till the word comes through. It's what they usually do."

He added as he closed the door, "And don't tell the fellows, or anybody, I've been talking to you. Okay, pal?"

"'Sure thing."

Alone again, Lucky pounded a fist slowly and softly into his palm. The Boss! Was that just talk? Scuttle-butt? Or did it mean something? And what about the rest of the conversation?

He had to wait. Galaxy! If only Conway and Henree had the good sense not to interfere for a while longer.


Lucky did not get a chance to view the "rock" as the *Atlas* approached. He did not see it until, preceded by Martin Maniu and followed by a second pirate, he stepped out of the air-lock into space and found it a hundred yards below.

The asteroid was quite typical. Lucky judged it to be two miles across the longest way. It was angular and craggy, as though a giant had torn off the top of a mountain and tossed it out into space. Its sunside glimmered gray-brown, and it was turning visibly, shadows shifting and changing.

He pushed downward toward the asteroid as he left the air-lock, flexing his leg muscles against the ship's hull. The crags floated up slowly toward him-self. When his hands touched ground, his inertia forced the rest of his body on downward, tumbling him in slowest motion until he could grasp a projection and bring himself to a halt.

He stood up. There was almost the illusion of a planetary surface about the rock. The nearest jags of matter, however, had nothing behind them, nothing but space. The stars, moving visibly as the rock turned, were hard, bright glitters. The ship, which had been put into an orbit about the rock, remained mo-tionless overhead.

A pirate led the way, some fifty feet, to a rise in

rock in no way distinguished from its surroundings. He made it in two long steps. As they waited a section of the rise slipped aside, and from the opening a space-suited figure stepped out.

"Okay, Herm," said one of the pirates, gruffly, "here he is. He's in your care now."

The voice that next sounded in Lucky's receiver was gentle and rather weary. "How long will he be with me, gentlemen?"

"Till we come to get him. And don't ask questions."

The pirates turned away and leaped upward. The rock's gravity could do nothing to stop them. They dwindled steadily and after a few minutes, Lucky saw a brief flash of crystals as one of them corrected his direction of travel by means of a push-gun; a small one, routinely used for such purposes, that was part of standard suit equipment. Its gas supply consisted of a built-in carbon dioxide cartridge.

Minutes passed and the ship's rear jets gleamed redly. It, too, began dwindling.

It was useless to try to check the direction in which it was leaving, Lucky knew, without some knowledge of his own location in space. And of that, except that he was somewhere in the asteroid belt, he knew nothing.

So intense was his absorption that he was almost startled at the soft voice of the other man on the asteroid.

He said, "It *is* beautiful out here. I come out so rarely that sometimes I forget. Look there!"

Lucky turned to his left. The small Sun was just poking above the sharp edge of the asteroid. In a moment it was too bright to look at. It was a gleaming twenty-credit gold piece. The sky, black before, remained black, and the stars shone undiminished. That was the way on an airless world where there was no dust to scatter sunlight and turn the heavens a deep, masking blue.

The man of the asteroid said, "In twenty-five minutes or so it will be setting again. Sometimes, when Jupiter is at its closest, you can see it, too, like a little marble, with its four satellites like sparks lined up in military formation. But that only happens every three and a half years. This isn't the time."

Lucky said bluntly, "Those men called you Herm. Is that your name? Are you one of them?"

"You mean am I a pirate? No. But I'll admit I may be an accessory after the fact. Nor is my name Herm. That's just a term they use for hermits in general. My name, sir, is Joseph Patrick Hansen, and since we are to be companions at close quarters for an indefinite period, I hope we shall be friends."

He held out a metal-sheathed hand, and Lucky grasped it.

"I'm Bill Williams," he said. "You say you're a hermit? Do you mean by that that you live here all the time?"

"That's right."

Lucky looked about the poor splinter of granite and silica and frowned. "It doesn't look very inviting."

"Nevertheless I'll try to do my best to make you comfortable."

The hermit touched a section of the slab or rock out of which he had come and a piece of it wheeled open once again. Lucky noted that the edges had been beveled and lined with lastium or some similar material to insure air tightness.

"Won't you step inside, Mr. Williams?" invited the hermit.

Lucky did so. The rock slab closed behind them. As it closed, a small Fluoro lit up and shone away the obscurity. It revealed a small air-lock, not much larger than was required to hold two men.

A small red signal light flickered, and the hermit said, "You can open your face-plate now. We've got air." He did so himself as he spoke.

Lucky followed suit, dragging in lungfuls of clear, fresh air. Not bad. Better than the air on shipboard. Definitely.

But it was when the inner door of the air-lock opened that the wind went out of Lucky in one big gasp.

# 6

## What the Hermit Knew

Lucky had seen few such luxurious rooms even on Earth. It was thirty feet long, twenty wide, and thirty high. A balcony circled it. Above and below the walls were lined with book films. A wall projector was set on a pedestal, while on another was a gemlike model of the Galaxy. The lighting was entirely indirect.

As soon as he set foot within the room, he felt the tug of a pseudo-grav motor. It wasn't set at Earth normal. From the feel of it it seemed somewhere between Earth and Mars normal. There was a delightful sensation of lightness and yet enough pull to allow full muscular coordination.

The hermit had removed his space-suit and suspended it over a white plastic trough into which the frost that had collected thickly over it when they stepped out of frozen space and into the warm, moist air of the room might trickle as it melted.

He was tall and straight, his face was pink and unlined, but his hair was quite white, as were his bushy eyebrows, and the veins stood out on the back of his hands.

He said politely, "May I help you with your suit?"

Lucky came to life. "That's all right." He clambered out quickly. "This is an unusual place you have here."

"You like it?" Hansen smiled. "It took many years to make it look like this. Nor is this all there is to my little home." He seemed filled with a quiet pride.

"I imagine so," said Lucky. "There must be a powerplant for light and heat as well as to keep the pseudo-grav field alive. You must have an air purifier and replacer, water supplies, food stores, all that."

"That's right."

"A hermit's life is not bad."

The hermit was obviously both proud and pleased. "It doesn't have to be," he said. "Sit down, Williams, sit down. Would you like a drink?"

"No, thank you." Lucky lowered himself into an armchair. Its apparently normal seat and back masked a soft diamagnetic field that gave under his weight only so far, then achieved a balance that molded itself to every curve of his body. "Unless you can scare up a cup of coffee?"

"Easily!" The old man stepped into an alcove. In seconds he was back with a fragrant and steaming cup, plus a second for himself.

The arm of Lucky's chair unfolded into a narrow ledge at the proper touch of Hansen's toe and the hermit set down one cup into an appropriate recess. As he did so he paused to stare at the younger man.

Lucky looked up. "Yes?"

Hansen shook his head. "Nothing. Nothing."

They faced one another. The lights in the more distant parts of the large room faded until only the area immediately surrounding the two men was clear to vision.

"And now if you'll pardon an old man's curiosity," said the hermit, "I'd like to ask you why you've come here."

"I didn't come. I was brought," said Lucky.

"You mean you're not one of——" Hansen paused.

"No, I'm not a pirate. At least, not yet."

Hansen put down his cup and looked troubled. "I don't understand. Perhaps I've said things I shouldn't have."

"Don't worry about it. I'm going to be one of them soon enough."

Lucky finished his coffee and then, choosing his words carefully, began with his boarding of the *Atlas* on the Moon and carried through to the moment.

Hansen listened in absorption. "And are you sure this is what you want to do, young man, now that you've seen a little of what life is like?"

"I'm sure."

"Why, for Earth's sake?"

"Exactly. For the sake of Earth and what it did to me. It's no place to live. Why did *you* come out here?"

"It's a long story, I'm afraid. You needn't look alarmed. I won't tell it. I bought this asteroid long ago as a place for small vacations, and I grew to like it. I kept enlarging the room space, brought furniture and book films from Earth little by little. Eventually I found I had all I needed here. So why not stay here permanently? I asked myself. And I did stay here permanently."

"Sure. Why not? You're smart. Back there it's a mess. Too many people. Too many rut jobs. Next to impossible to get out to the planets, and if you do, it means a job of manual labor. No opportunity for a man any more unless he comes to the asteroids. I'm not old enough to settle down like you. But for a young fellow it's a free life and an exciting one. There's room to be boss."

"The ones who are already boss don't like young fellows with boss notions in their head. Anton, for instance. I've seen him and I know."

"Maybe, but so far he's kept his word," said Lucky. "He said if I came out winner over this Dingo, I'd have my chance to join the men of the asteroids. It looks as though I'm getting the chance."

"It looks as though you're here, that's all. What if he returns with proof, or what he calls proof, that you're a government man?"

"He won't."

"And if he does? Just to get rid of you?"

Lucky's face darkened and again Hansen looked at him curiously, frowning a bit.

Lucky said, "He wouldn't. He can use a good man and he knows it. Besides, why are you preaching to me? You're out here yourself playing ball with them."

Hansen looked down. "It's true. I shouldn't interfere with you. It's just that being alone here so long, I'm apt to talk too much when a person does come along, just to hear the sound of voices. Look, it's about time for dinner. I would be glad to have you eat with me in silence, if you'd rather. Or else we'll talk about anything you choose."

"Well, thanks, Mr. Hansen. No hard feelings."

"Good."

Lucky followed Hansen through a door into a small pantry lined with canned food and concentrates of all sorts. None of the brand names familiar to Lucky were represented. Instead the contents of each can were described in brightly colored etchings that were themselves integral parts of the metal.

Hansen said, "I used to keep meat in a special freeze room. You can get the temperature down all the way on an asteroid, you know, but it's been two years since I could get that kind of supplies."

He chose half a dozen cans off the shelves, plus a container of milk concentrate. At his suggestion Lucky took up a sealed gallon container of water from a lower shelf.

The hermit set the table quickly. The cans were of the self-heating type that opened up into dishes with enclosed cutlery.

Hansen said, with some amusement, indicating the cans, "I've got a whole valley on the outside brim-filled with these things. Discarded ones, that is. A twenty years' accumulation."

The food was good, but strange. It was yeast-base material, the kind only the Terrestrial Empire produced. Nowhere else in the Galaxy was the pressure of population so great, the billions of people so numerous, that yeast culture had been developed. On Venus, where most of the yeast products were grown, almost any variety of food imitation could be produced: steaks, nuts, butter, candy. It was as nourishing as the real thing, too. To Lucky, however, the flavor was not quite Venusian. There was a sharper tang to it.

"Pardon me for being nosy," he said, "but all this takes money, doesn't it?"

"Oh yes, and I have some. I have investments on Earth. Quite good ones. My checks are always honored, or at least they were until not quite two years ago."

"What happened then?"

"The supply ships stopped coming. Too risky on account of the pirates. It was a bad blow. I had a good backlog of supplies in most things, but I can imagine how it must have been for the others."

"The others?"

"The other hermits. There are hundreds of us. They're not all as lucky as I am. Very few can afford to make their worlds quite this comfortable, but they can manage the essentials. It's usually old people like myself, with wives dead, children grown up, the world strange and different, who go off by themselves. If they have a little nest egg, they can get a little asteroid started. The government doesn't charge. Any asteroid you want to settle on, if it's less than five miles in diameter, is yours. Then if they want they can invest in a sub-etheric receiver and keep up with the universe. If not, they can have book films, or can arrange to have news transcripts brought in by the supply ships once a year, or they can just eat, rest, sleep, and wait to die if they'd rather. I wish, sometimes, I'd got to know some of them."

"Why haven't you?"

"Sometimes I've felt willing, but they're not easy

people to know. After all, they've come here to be alone, and for that matter, so have I."

"Well, what did you do when the supply ships stopped coming?"

"Nothing at first. I thought surely the government would clean up the situation and I had enough supplies for months. In fact, I could have skimped along a year, maybe. But then the pirate ships came."

"And you threw in with them?"

The hermit shrugged. His eyebrows drew together in a troubled frown and they finished their meal in silence.

At the end he gathered the can plates and cutlery and placed them in a wall container in the alcove that led to the pantry. Lucky heard a dim grating noise of metal on metal that diminished rapidly.

Hansen said, "The pseudo-grav field doesn't extend to the disposal tube. A puff of air and they sail out to the valley I told you of, even though it's nearly a mile away."

"It seems to me," said Lucky, "that if you'd try a little harder puff, you'd get rid of the cans altogether."

"So I would. I think most hermits do that. Maybe they all do. I don't like the idea, though. It's a waste of air, and of metal too. We might reclaim those cans someday. Who knows? Besides, even though most of the cans would scatter here and there, I'm sure that some would circle this asteroid like little moons and it's undignified to think of being accompanied on your orbit by your garbage. Care to smoke? No? Mind if I do?"

He lit a cigar and with a contented sigh went on.

"The men of the asteroids can't supply tobacco regularly, so this is becoming a rare treat for me."

Lucky said, "Do they furnish you the rest of your supplies?"

"That's right. Water, machine parts and power-pack renewals. It's an arrangement."

"And what do you do for them?"

The hermit studied his cigar's lighted end. "Not much. They use this world. They land their ships on it and I don't report them. They don't come in here and what they do elsewhere on the rock isn't my business. I don't want to know. It's safer that way. Men are left here sometimes, like yourself, and are picked up later. I have an idea they stop for minor repairs sometimes. They bring me supplies in return."

"Do they supply all the hermits?"

"I wouldn't know. Maybe."

"It would take an awful lot of supplies. Where would they get them from?"

"They capture ships."

"Not enough to supply hundreds of hermits *and* themselves. I mean, it would take an awful lot of ships."

"I wouldn't know."

"Aren't you interested? It's a soft life you have here, but maybe the food we just ate came off a ship whose crew are frozen corpses circling some other asteroid like human garbage. Do you ever think of that?"

The hermit flushed painfully. "You're getting your revenge for my having preached to you earlier. You're right, but what can I do? I didn't abandon or betray the government. They abandoned and betrayed me. My estate on Earth pays taxes. Why am I not protected then? I registered this asteroid with the Terrestrial Outer World Bureau in good faith. It's part of the Terrestrial dominion. I have every right to expect protection against the pirates. If that's not forthcoming; if my source of supply coolly says that they can bring me nothing more at any price, what am I supposed to do?

"You might say I could have returned to Earth, but how could I abandon all this? I have a world of my own here. My book films, the great classics that I love. I even have a copy of Shakespeare; a direct filming of the actual pages of an ancient printed book. I have food, drink, privacy: I could find nowhere as confortable as this anywhere else in the Universe.

"Don't think it's been an easy choice, though. I have a sub-etheric transmitter. I could communicate with Earth. I've got a little ship that can make the short haul to Ceres. The men of the asteroids know that, but they trust me. They know I have no choice. As I told you when we first met, I'm an accessory after the fact.

"I've helped them. That makes me legally a pirate. It would be jail, execution, probably, if I return. If not, if they free me provided I turn state's evidence, the men of the asteroids won't forget. They would find me no matter where I went, unless I could be guaranteed complete government protection for life."

"It looks like you're in a bad way," said Lucky.

"Am I?" said the hermit. "I might be able to get that complete protection with the proper help."

It was Lucky's turn. "I wouldn't know," he said.

"I think you would."

"I don't get you."

"Look, I'll give you a word of warning in return for help."

"There's nothing *I* can do. What's your word?"

"Get off the asteroid before Anton and his men come back."

"Not on your life. I came here to join them, not to go home."

"If you don't leave, you'll stay forever. You'll stay as a dead man. They won't let you on any crew. You won't qualify, mister."

Lucky's face twisted in anger. "What in space are you talking about, old-timer?"

"There it is again. When you get angry, I see it plainly. You're not Bill Williams, son. What's your relationship to Lawrence Starr of the Council of Science? Are you Starr's son?"

# 7

## To Ceres

Lucky's eyes narrowed. He felt the muscles of his right arm tense as though to reach for a hip at which no blaster nestled. He made no actual motion.

His voice remained under strict control. He said, "Whose son? What are you talking about?"

"I'm sure of it." The hermit leaned forward, seizing Lucky's wrist earnestly. "I knew Lawrence Starr well. He was my friend. He helped me once when I needed help. And you're his image. I couldn't be wrong."

Lucky pulled his hand away. "You're not making sense."

"Listen, son, it may be important to you not to give away your identity. Maybe you don't trust me. All right, I'm not telling you to trust me. I've been working with the pirates and I've admitted it. But listen to me anyway. The men of the asteroids have a good organization. It may take them weeks, but if Anton suspects you, they won't stop till you're checked from the ground up. No phony story will fool them. They'll get the truth and they'll learn who

71

you are. Be sure of that! They'll get your true identity. Leave, I tell you. Leave!"

Lucky said, "If I were this guy you say I am, old-timer, aren't you getting yourself into trouble? I take it you want me to use your ship."

"Yes."

"And what would *you* do when the pirates returned?"

"I wouldn't be here. Don't you see? I want to go with you."

"And leave all you have here?"

The old man hesitated. "Yes, it's hard. But I won't have a chance like this again. You're a man of influence; you must be. You're a member of the Council of Science, perhaps. You're here on secret work. They'll believe you. You could protect me, vouch for me. You would prevent prosecution, see that no harm came to me from the pirates. It would pay the Council, young man. I would tell them all I know about the pirates. I would co-operate in every way I could."

Lucky said, "Where do you keep your ship?"

"It's a deal, then?"

The ship was a small one indeed. The two reached it through a narrow corridor, walking single file, their figures grotesque again in space-suits.

Lucky said, "Is Ceres close enough to pick out by ship's telescope?"

"Yes indeed."

"You could recognize it without trouble?"

"Certainly."

"Let's get on board, then."

The fore end of the airless cavern that housed the

ship opened outward as soon as the ship's motors were activated.

"Radio control," explained Hansen.

The ship was fueled and provisioned. It worked smoothly, rising out of its berth and into space with the ease and freedom possible only where gravitational forces were virtually lacking. For the first time Lucky saw Hansen's asteroid from space. He caught a glimpse of the valley of the discarded cans, brighter than the surrounding rock, just before it passed into shadow.

Hansen said, "Tell me, now. You are the son of Lawrence Starr, aren't you?"

Lucky had located a well-charged blaster and a holster belt to boot. He was strapping it on as he spoke.

"My name," he said, "is David Starr. Most people call me Lucky."

Ceres is a monster among the asteroids. It is nearly five hundred miles in diameter, and, standing upon it, the average man actually weighs two full pounds. It is quite spherical in shape, and anyone very close to it in space could easily think it was a respectable planet.

Still, if the Earth were hollow, it would be possible to throw into it four thousand bodies the size of Ceres before filling it up.

Bigman stood on the surface of Ceres, his figure bloated in a space-suit which had been loaded to bursting with lead weights and on shoes the soles of which were foot-thick lead clogs. It had been his own idea, but it was quite useless. He still weighed less than four pounds and his every motion threatened to twist him up into space.

He had been on Ceres for days now, since the quick space flight with Conway and Henree from the Moon, waiting for this moment, waiting for Lucky Starr to send in the radio message that he was coming in. Gus Henree and Hector Conway had been nervous about it, fearing Lucky's death, worrying about it. He, Bigman, had known better. Lucky could come through anything. He told them that. When Lucky's message finally came, he told them again.

But just the same, out here on Ceres' frozen soil with nothing between himself and the stars, he admitted a sneaking sensation of relief.

From where he sat he was looking directly at the dome of the Observatory, its lower reaches dipping just a little below the close horizon. It was the largest observatory in the Terrestrial Empire for a very logical reason.

In that part of the Solar System inside the orbit of Jupiter, the planets Venus, Earth, and Mars had atmospheres and were by that very fact poorly suited for astronomic observation. The interfering air, even when it was as thin as that of Mars, blotted out the finer detail. It wavered and flickered star images and spoiled things generally.

The largest airless object inside Jupiter's orbit was Mercury, but that was so close to the Sun that the observatory in its twilight zone specialized in solar observations. Relatively small telescopes sufficed.

The second largest airless object was the Moon. Here again circumstances dictated specialization. Weather forecasts on Earth, for instance, had become an accurate, long-range science, since the appearance of Earth's atmosphere could be viewed as a whole from a distance of a quarter of a million miles.

And the third largest airless object was Ceres, and that was the best of the three. Its almost nonexistent gravity allowed huge lenses and mirrors to be poured without the danger of breakage, without even the question of sag, due to its own weight. The structure of the telescope tube itself needed no particular strength. Ceres was nearly three times as far from the Sun as was the Moon and sunlight was only one eighth as strong. Its rapid revolution kept Ceres' temperature almost constant. In short, Ceres was ideal for observation of the stars and of the outer planets.

Only the day before Bigman had seen Saturn through the thousand-inch reflecting telescope, the grinding of the huge mirror having consumed twenty years of painstaking and continuous labor.

"What do I look through?" he had asked.

They laughed at him. "You don't look through anything," they said.

They worked the controls carefully, three of them, each doing something that co-ordinated with the other two, until all were satisfied. The dim red lights dimmed further and in the pit of black emptiness about which they sat a blob of light sprang into being. A touch at the controls and it focused sharply.

Bigman whistled his astonishment. It was Saturn!

It was Saturn, three feet wide, exactly as he had seen it from space half a dozen times. Its triple rings were bright and he could see three marble-like moons. Behind it was a numerous dusting of stars. Bigman wanted to walk about it to see how it looked with the night shadow cutting it, but the picture didn't change as he moved.

"It's just an image," they told him, "an illusion. You see the same thing no matter where you stand."

Now, from the asteroid's surface, Bigman could spot Saturn with the naked eye. It was just a white dot, but brighter than the other white dots that were the stars. It was twice as bright as it appeared from Earth, since it was two hundred million miles closer here. Earth itself was on the other side of Ceres near the pea-size Sun. Earth wan't a very impressive sight, since the Sun invariably dwarfed it.

Bigman's helmet suddenly rang with sound as the call flooded his left-open radio receiver.

"Hey, Shortie, get moving. There's a ship coming in."

Bigman jumped at the noise and moved straight upward, limbs flailing. He yelled, "Who're you calling Shortie?"

But the other was laughing. "Hey, how much do you charge for flying lessons, little boy?"

"I'll little boy you," screamed Bigman furiously. He had reached the peak of his parabola and was slowly and hesitatingly beginning to settle downward once more. "What's your name, wise guy? Say your name, and I'll crack your gizzard as soon as I get back and peel the suit."

"Think you can reach my gizzard?" came the mocking rejoinder, and Bigman would have exploded into tiny pieces if he had not caught sight of a ship slanting down from the horizon.

He loped in giant, clumsy strides about the leveled

square mile of ground that was the asteroid's space-port, trying to judge the exact spot on which the ship would land.

It dropped down its steaming jets to a feather-touch planetary contact and when the air-locks opened and Lucky's tall, suited figure emerged, Bigman, yelling his joy, made one long leap of it, and they were to-gether.

Conway and Henree were less effusive in their wel-come, but no less joyful. Each wrung Lucky's hand as though to confirm, by sheer muscular pressure, the reality of the flesh and blood they beheld.

Lucky laughed. "Whoa, will you? Give me a chance to breathe. What's the matter? Didn't you think I was coming back?"

"Look here," said Conway, "you'd better consult us before you take off on just any old fool notion."

"Well, now, not if it's too much of a fool notion, please, or you won't let me."

"Never mind that. I can ground you for what you've done. I can have you put under detention right now. I can suspend you. I can throw you off the Council," said Conway.

"Which of them are you going to do?"

"None of them, you darned overgrown young fool. But I *may* beat your brains out one of these days."

Lucky turned to Augustus Henree. "You won't let him, will you?"

"Frankly, I'll help him."

"Then I give up in advance. Look, there's a gentle-man here I'd like to have you meet."

Until now Hansen had remained in the background,

obviously amused by the interchange of nonsense. The two older Councilmen had been too full of Lucky Starr even to be aware of his existence.

"Dr. Conway," said Lucky, "Dr. Henree, this is Mr. Joseph P. Hansen, the man whose ship I used to come back. He has been of considerable assistance to me."

The old hermit shook hands with the two scientists.

"I don't suppose you can possibly know Drs. Conway and Henree," said Lucky. The hermit shook his head.

"Well," he went on, "they're important officials in the Council of Science. After you've eaten and had a chance to rest, they'll talk to you and help you, I'm sure."

An hour later the two Councilmen faced Lucky with somber expressions. Dr. Henree tamped tobacco into his pipe with a little finger, and smoked quietly as he listened to Lucky's accounts of his adventures with the pirates.

"Have you told this to Bigman?" he asked.

"I've just spent some time talking to him," said Lucky.

"And he didn't assault you for not taking him?"

"He wasn't pleased," Lucky admitted.

But Conway's mind was more seriously oriented. "A Sirian-designed ship, eh?" he mused.

"Undoubtedly so," said Lucky. "At least we have that piece of information."

"The information wasn't worth the risk," said Conway, dryly. "I'm much more disturbed over another piece of information we have now. It's obvious that the Sirian organization penetrates into the Council of Science itself."

Henree nodded gravely. "Yes, I saw that, too. Very bad."

Lucky said, "How do you make that out?"

"Galaxy, boy, it's obvious," growled Conway. "I'll admit that we had a large construction crew working on the ship and that even with the best intentions careless slips of information can take place. It remains truth, though, that the fact of the booby-trapping and particularly the exact manner of the fusing were known only to Council members and not too many of those. Somewhere in that small group is a spy, yet I could have sworn that all were faithful." He shook his head. "I still can't believe otherwise."

"You don't have to," said Lucky.

"Oh? And why not?"

"Because the Sirian contact was quite temporary. The Sirian Embassy got their information from *me*."

# 8

## Bigman Takes Over

"Indirectly, of course, through one of their known spies," he amplified, as the two older men stared at him in shocked astonishment.

"I don't understand you at all," said Henree in a low voice. Conway was obviously speechless.

"It was necessary. I had to introduce myself to the pirates without suspicion. If they found me on what they thought was a mapping ship, they would have shot me out of hand. On the other hand, if they found me on a bobby-trapped ship the secret of which they had stumbled on by what seemed a stroke of fortune, they would have taken me at face value as a stowaway. Don't you see? On a mapping ship I'm only a member of the crew that didn't get away in time. On a booby trap, I'm a poor jerk who didn't realize what he was stowing away on."

"They might have shot you anyway. They might have seen through your double-cross and considered you a spy. In fact, they almost did."

"True! They almost did," admitted Lucky.

Conway finally exploded. "And what about the

original plan? Were we or were we not going to explode one of their bases? When I consider the months we spent on the construction of the *Atlas,* the money that went into it—"

"What good would it have done to explode one of their bases? We spoke about a huge hangar of pirate ships, but actually that was only wishful thinking. An organization based upon the asteroids would have to be decentralized. The pirates probably don't have more than three or four ships in any one place. There wouldn't be room for more. Exploding three or four ships would mean very little compared with what would have been accomplished if I had succeeded in penetrating their organization."

"But you didn't succeed," said Conway. "With all your fool risks, you didn't succeed."

"Unfortunately the pirate captain who took the *Atlas* was too suspicious, or perhaps too intelligent for us. I'll try not to underestimate them again. But it's not all loss. We know for a fact that Sirius is behind them. In addition, we have my hermit friend."

"He won't help us," said Conway. "From what you've said about him, it sounds as though he were only interested in having as little to do with the pirates as possible. So what can he know?"

"He may be able to tell us more than he himself thinks is possible," said Lucky coolly. "For instance, there's one piece of information he can give us that will enable me to continue efforts at working against piracy from the inside."

"You're not going out there again," said Conway hastily.

"I don't intend to," said Lucky.

Conway's eyes narrowed. "Where's Bigman?"

"On Ceres. Don't worry. In fact," and a shadow crossed Lucky's face, "he should be here by now. The delay is beginning to bother me a little."

John Bigman Jones used his special pass card to get past the guard at the door to the Control Tower. He was muttering to himself as he half-ran along the corridors.

The slight flush on his pug-nosed face dimmed his freckles and his reddish hair stood up in tufts like fence pickets. Lucky had frequently told him he cultivated a vertical hair-do to make himself look taller, but he always denied that vigorously.

The final door to the Tower swung open as he broke the photoelectric beam. He stepped inside and looked about.

Three men were on duty. One with earphones sat at the sub-etheric receiver, another was at the calculating machine and the third was at the curved radarized visiplate.

Bigman said, "Which one of you knotbrains called me Shortie?"

The three turned toward him in unison, their faces startled and scowling.

The man with the earphones pulled one away from his left ear. "Who in space are you? How the dickens did you get in here?"

Bigman stood erect and puffed out his small chest. "My name is John Bigman Jones. My friends call me Bigman. Everyone else calls me Mr. Jones. Nobody calls me Shortie and stays in one piece. I want to know which one of you made that mistake."

The man with the earphones said, "My name is Lem Fisk and you can call me anything you blame please as long as you do it somewhere else. Get out of here, or I'll come down, pick you up by one leg, and toss you out."

The fellow at the calculating machine said, "Hey, Lem, that's the crackpot who was haunting the port a while back. There's no point in wasting time on him. Get the guards to throw him out."

"Nuts," said Lem Fisk, "we don't need guards for that guy."

He took off his earphones altogether and set the sub-etherics at AUTOMATIC SIGNAL. He said, "Well, son, you came in here and asked us a nice question in a nice way. I'll give you a nice answer. I called you Shortie, but wait, don't get mad. I have a reason. You see you're such a real tall fellow. You're such a long drink of water. You're such a high-pockets. It makes my friends laugh to hear me call you Shortie."

He reached into his hip pocket and drew out a plastic container of cigarettes. The smile on his face was bland.

"Come down here," yelled Bigman. "Come down here and back up your sense of humor with a couple of fists."

"Temper, temper," said Fisk, clucking his tongue. "Here, boy, have a cigarette. King-size, you know. Almost as long as you are. Liable to create some confusion, though, come to think of it. We won't be able to tell whether you're smoking the cigarette or the cigarette is smoking you."

The other two Tower men laughed vigorously.

Bigman was a passionate red. Words came thickly to his tongue. "You won't fight?"

"I'd rather smoke. Pity you don't join me." Fisk leaned back, chose a cigarette, and held it before his face as though admiring its slim whiteness. "After all, I can't be bothered to fight children."

He grinned, brought his cigarette to his lips, and found them closing on nothingness.

His thumb and first two fingers still held their positions about three eighths of an inch apart, but there was no cigarette between them.

"Watch out, Lem," cried the man at the visiplate. "He has a needle-gun."

"No needle-gun," snarled Bigman. "Just a buzzer."

There was an important difference. A buzzer's projectiles, although needle-like, were fragile and nonexplosive. They were used for target practice and small game. Striking human skin, a buzz needle would do no serious damage, but it would smart like the devil.

Fisk's grin disappeared completely. He yelled, "Watch that, you crazy fool. You can blind a man with that."

Bigman's fist remained clenched at eye level. The thin snout of the buzzer projected between his two middle fingers. He said, "I won't blind you. But I can fix it so you won't sit down for a month. And as you can see, my aim isn't bad. And you," he called over his shoulder to the one at the calculator, "if you move an inch closer to the alarm circuit, you'll have a buzz needle right through your hand."

Fisk said, "What do you want?"

"Come down here and fight."

"Against a buzzer?"

"I'll put it away. Fists. Fair fight. Your buddies can see to that."

"I can't hit a guy smaller than I am."

"Then you shouldn't insult him, either." Bigman brought up the buzzer. "And I'm not smaller than you are. I may look that way on the outside, but inside I'm as big as you. Maybe bigger. I'm counting three." He narrowed one eye as he aimed.

"Galaxy!" swore Fisk. "I'm coming down. Fellas, be my witness that this was forced on me. I'll try not to hurt the crazy idiot too much."

He leaped down from his perch. The man at the calculating machine took his place at the sub-etherics.

Fisk was five feet ten, eight inches taller than Bigman, whose slight figure was more like a boy's than a man's. But Bigman's muscles were steel springs under perfect control. He waited for the other's approach without expression.

Fisk did not bother to put up a guard. He simply extended his right hand as though he were going to lift Bigman by the collar and toss him through the still open door.

Bigman ducked under the arm. His left and right thudded into the larger man's solar plexus in a rapid one-two, and almost in the same instant he danced out of reach.

Fisk turned green and sat down, holding his stomach and groaning.

"Stand up, big boy," said Bigman. "I'll wait for you."

The other two Tower men seemed frozen into immobility by the sudden turn of events.

Slowly Fisk rose to his feet. His face glowed with rage, but he approached more slowly.

Bigman drifted away.

Fisk lunged! Bigman was not there by two inches. Fisk whipped a sharp overhand right. Its thrust ended an inch short of Bigman's jaw.

Bigman bobbed about like a cork on rippling water. His arms lifted occasionally to deflect a blow.

Fisk, yelling incoherently, rushed blindly at his gnat-like opponent. Bigman stepped to one side and his open hand slapped sharply at the other's smooth-shaven cheek. It hit with a sharp report, like a meteor hitting the first layers of dense air above a planet. The marks of four fingers were outlines on Fisk's face.

For a moment Fisk stood there, dazed. Like a striking snake, Bigman stepped in again, his fists moving upward to crack against Fisk's jaw. Fisk went down into a half crouch.

Distantly Bigman was suddenly aware of the steady ringing of the alarm.

Without a moment's hesitation he turned on his heel and was out the door. He wove through a startled trio of guards heading up the corridor at a clattering run, and was gone!

"And why," questioned Conway, "are we waiting for Bigman?"

Lucky said, "Here's the way I see the situation. There is nothing we need so badly as more information about the pirates. I mean inside information. I tried to get it and things didn't quite break the way I hoped they would. I'm a marked man now. They know me.

But they don't know Bigman. He has no official connection with the Council. Now it's my idea that if we can trump up a criminal charge against him, for realism, you know, he can hightail it out of Ceres in the hermit's ship——"

"Oh, space," groaned Conway.

"Listen, will you! He'll go back to the hermit's asteroid. If the pirates are there, good! If not, he'll leave the ship in plain view and wait for them inside. It's a very comfortable place to wait in."

"And when they come," said Henree, "they'll shoot him."

"They will *not*. That's why he's taking the hermit's ship. They'll have to know where Hansen went, to say nothing of myself, where Bigman came from, how he got hold of the ship. They'll *have* to know. That will give him time to talk."

"And to explain how he picked out Hansen's asteroid out of all the rocks in creation? That would take some tall talking."

"That won't take any talking at all. The hermit's ship was on Ceres, which it is. I've arranged to leave it out there unguarded, so he can take it. He'll find the ship's home asteroid's space-time co-ordinates in the log-book. It would just be an asteroid to him, not too far from Ceres, as good as any other, and he would make a beeline for it in order to wait for the furor on Ceres to die down."

"It's a risk," grumbled Conway.

"Bigman knows it. And I tell you right now, we've *got* to take risks. Earth is underestimating the pirate menace so badly that ——"

He interrupted himself as the signal light of the

Communi-tube flashed on and off in rapid dots of light.

Conway, with an impatient motion of his hand, cut in the signal analyzer, then sat up straight.

He said, "It's on the Council wave length and, by Ceres, it's one of the Council scramblings."

The small visiplate above the Communi-tube was showing a characteristic rapidly shifting pattern of light and dark.

Conway inserted a sliver of metal, which he took from a group of such in his wallet, into a narrow slot in the Communi-tube. The sliver was a crystallite unscrambler, the active portion of the gadget consisting of a particular pattern of tiny crystals of tungsten embedded in an alumimum matrix. It filtered the sub-etheric signal in a specific way. Slowly Conway adjusted the unscrambler, pushing it in deeper and extracting it again until it matched exactly a scrambler similar in nature but opposite in function, at the other end of the signal.

The moment of complete adjustment was heralded by the sudden sharp focusing of the visiplate.

Lucky half-rose to his feet. "Bigman!" he said. "Where in space are you?"

Bigman's little face was grinning puckishly out at them. "I'm in space all right. A hundred thousand miles off Ceres. I'm in the hermit's ship."

Conway whispered furiously, "Is this another of your tricks? I though you said he was on Ceres?"

"I thought he was," Lucky said. Then, "What happened, Bigman?"

"You said we had to act quickly, so I fixed things up myself. One of the wise guys in the Control

Tower was giving me the business. So I slammed him around a little and took off." He laughed. "Check the guardhouse and see if they're not on the lookout for a guy like me with a complaint of assault and battery against him."

"That wasn't the brightest thing you could have done," said Lucky gravely. "You'll have a hard time convincing the men of the asteroids that you're the type for assault. I don't want to hurt your feelings, but you look a little small for the job."

"I'll knock down a few," Bigman retorted. "They'll believe me. But that's not why I called."

"Well, why did you?"

"How do I get to this guy's asteroid?"

Lucky frowned. "Have you looked in the log-book?"

"Great Galaxy! I've looked everywhere. I've looked under the mattress even. There's no record anywhere of any kind of co-ordinates."

Lucky's look of uneasiness grew. "That's strange. In fact it's worse than strange. Look, Bigman," he spoke rapidly and incisively, "match Ceres' speed. Give me your co-ordinates with respect to Ceres right now and keep them that way, whatever you do, till I call you. You're too close to Ceres now for any pirates to bother you, but if you drift out further, you may be in a bad way. Do you hear me?"

"Check. Got you. Let me calculate my co-ordinates."

Lucky wrote them down and broke connections. He said, "Space, when will I learn *not* to make assumptions."

Henree said, "Hadn't you better have Bigman

come back? It's a foolhardy setup at best and as long as you haven't the co-ordinates, give the whole thing up."

"Give it up?" said Lucky. "Give up the one asteroid we know to be a pirates' base? Do you know of any other? One single other? We've got to find the asteroid. It's our only clue to the inside of this knot."

Conway said, "He's got a point there, Gus. It is a base."

Lucky jiggled a switch on the intercom briskly and waited.

Hansen's voice, sleep-filled but startled, said, "Hello! Hello!"

Lucky said briskly, "This is Lucky Starr, Mr. Hansen. Sorry to disturb you, but I would like to have you come down here to Dr. Conway's room as fast as you can."

The hermit's voice answered after a pause, "Certainly, but I don't know the way."

"The guard at your door will take you. I'll contact him. Can you make it in two minutes?"

"Two and a half anyway," he said, good-humoredly. He sounded more awake.

"Good enough!"

Hansen was as good as his word. Lucky was waiting for him.

Lucky paused for a moment, holding the door open. He said to the guard, "Has there been any trouble at the base earlier this evening? An assault, perhaps?"

The guard looked surprised. "Yes, sir. The man who got hurt refused to press charges, though. Claimed it was a fair fight."

Lucky closed the door. He said, "That follows. Any normal man would hate to get up in a guardhouse and admit a fellow the size of Bigman had given him a banging. I'll call the authorities later and have them put the charge on paper anyway. For the record. . . . Mr. Hansen."

"Yes, Mr. Starr?"

"I have a question the answer to which I did not want floating around this intercom system. Tell me, what are the co-ordinates of your home asteroid? Standard and temporal both, of course."

Hansen stared and his china-blue eyes grew round. "Well, you may find this hard to believe, but do you know, I really couldn't tell you."

# 9

## The Asteroid That Wasn't

Lucky met his eye steadily. "That is hard to believe, Mr. Hansen. I should think you would know your co-ordinates as well as a planet dweller would know his home address."

The hermit looked at his toes and said mildly, "I suppose so. It *is* my home address, really. Yet I don't know it."

Conway said, "If this man is deliberately——"

Lucky broke in. "Now wait. Let's force patience on ourselves if we have to. Mr. Hansen must have some explanation."

They waited for the hermit to speak.

Co-ordinates of the various bodies in the Galaxy were the lifeblood of space travel. They fulfilled the same function that lines of latitude and longitude did on the two-dimensional surface of a planet. However, since space is three-dimensional, and since the bodies in it move about in every possible way, the necessary co-ordinates are more complicated.

Basically there is first a standard zero position. In the case of the Solar System, the Sun was the usual standard. Based on that standard, three numbers are necessary. The first number is the distance of an object or a position in space from the Sun. The second and third numbers are two angular measurements indicating the position of the object with reference to an imaginary line connecting the Sun and the center of the Galaxy. If three sets of such co-ordinates are known for three different times, set well apart, the orbit of a moving body could be calculated and its position, relative to the Sun, known for any given time.

Ships could calculate their own co-ordinates with respect to the Sun or, if it were more convenient, with respect to the nearest large body, whatever it was. On the Lunar Lines, for instance, of which vessels traveled from Earth to the Moon and back, Earth was the customary "zero point." The Sun's own co-ordinates could be calculated with respect to the Galactic Center and the Galactic Prime Meridian, but that was only important in traveling between the stars.

Some of all this might have been passing through the hermit's mind as he sat there with the three Councilmen watching him narrowly. It was hard to tell.

Hansen said suddenly, "Yes, I can explain."

"We're waiting," said Lucky.

"I've never had occasion to use the co-ordinates in fifteen years. I haven't left my asteroid at all for two years and before that any trips I made, maybe one or two a year, were short ones to Ceres or Vesta for supplies of one sort or another. When I did that, I used local co-ordinates which I always calculated out for the moment. I never worked out a table because I didn't have to.

"I'd only be gone a day or two, three at the most, and my own rock wouldn't drift far in that time. It travels with the stream, a little slower than Ceres or Vesta when it's further from the Sun and a little faster when it's nearer. When I'd head back for the position I calculated, my rock might have drifted ten thousand or even a hundred thousand miles off its original spot, but it was always close enough to pick up with the ship's telescope. After that, I could always adjust my course by eye. I never used the solar standard co-ordinates because I never had to, and there it is."

"What you're saying," said Lucky, "is that you couldn't get back to your rock now. Or did you calculate its local co-ordinates before you left?"

"I never thought to," said the hermit sadly. "It's been so long since I left it that I never gave the matter a second's attention. Not until the minute you called me in here."

Dr. Henree said, "Wait. Wait." He had lit up a fresh pipeful of tobacco and was puffing strongly. "I may be wrong, Mr. Hansen, but when you first took over ownership of your asteroid, you must have filed a claim with the Terrestrial Outer World Bureau. Is that right?"

"Yes," said Hansen, "but it was only a formality."

"That could be. I'm not arguing that. Still, the co-ordinates of your asteroid would be on record there."

Hansen thought a bit, then shook his head. "I'm afraid not, Dr. Henree. They took only the standard co-ordinate set for January 1 of that year. That was just to identify the asteroid, like a code number, in case of disputed ownership. They weren't interested in anything more than that and you can't compute an orbit from only one set of numbers."

"But you yourself must have had orbital values. Lucky told us that you first used the asteroid as an annual vacation spot. So you must have been able to find it from year to year."

"That was fifteen years ago, Dr. Henree. I *had* the values, yes. And those values are somewhere in my record books on the rock, but they're not in my memory."

Lucky, his brown eyes clouded, said, "There's nothing else at the moment, Mr. Hansen. The guard will take you back to the room and we'll let you know when we need you again. And, Mr. Hansen," he added as the hermit rose, "if you should happen to think of the co-ordinates, let us know."

"My word on that, Mr. Starr," said Hansen gravely.

The three were alone again. Lucky's hand shot out to the Communi-tube. "Key me in for transmission," he said.

The voice of the man at Central Communications came back. "Was the previous incoming message for you, sir? I couldn't unscramble it so I thought——"

"You did well. Transmission, please."

Lucky adjusted a scrambler and used Bigman's co-ordinates to zero in the sub-etheric beam.

"Bigman," he said when the other's face appeared, "open the logbook again."

"Do you have the co-ordinates, Lucky?"

"Not yet. Have you got the logbook open?"

"Yes."

"Is there a sheet of scrap paper somewhere in it? Loose, with calculations all over it?"

"Wait. Yes. Here it is."

"Hold it up in front of your transmitter. I want to see it."

Lucky pulled a sheet of paper before him and copied down the figuring. "All right, Bigman, take it away. Now listen, stay put. Get me? Stay put, no matter what, till you hear from me. Signing off."

He turned to the two older men. "I navigated the ship from the hermit's rock to Ceres by eye. I adjusted course three or four times, using his ship's telescope and vernier instruments for observation and measurements. These are my calculations."

Conway nodded. "Now, I suppose, you intend calculating backwards to find out the rock's coordinates."

"It can be done easily enough, particularly if we make use of the Ceres Observatory."

Conway rose heavily. "I can't help but think you make too much of all this, but I'll follow your instinct for a while. Let's go to the Observatory."

Corridors and elevators took them close to Ceres' surface, one half mile above the Council of Science offices on the asteroid. It was chilly there, since the Observatory made every attempt to keep the temperature as constant as possible and as near surface temperature as the human body could endure.

Slowly and carefully a young technician was unraveling Lucky's calculations, feeding them into the computer and controlling the operations.

Dr. Henree, in a not too comfortable chair, huddled his thin body together and seemed to be trying to extract warmth from his pipe, for his large-knuckled hands hovered closely about its bowl.

He said, "I hope this comes to something."

Lucky said, "It had better." He sat back, his eyes fixed thoughtfully on the opposite wall. "Look, Uncle Hector, you referred to my 'instinct' a while back. It isn't instinct; not any more. This run of piracy is entirely different from that of a quarter century ago."

"Their ships are harder to catch or stop, if that's what you mean," said Conway.

"Yes, but doesn't that make it all the stranger that their raids are confined to the asteroid belt? It's only here in the asteroids that trade has been disrupted."

"They're being cautious. Twenty-five years ago, when their ships ranged all the way to Venus, we were forced to mount an offensive and crush them. Now they stick to the asteroids and the government hesitates to take expensive measures."

"So far, so good," said Lucky, "but how do they support themselves? It's always been the assumption that pirates didn't raid for pure joy of it alone, but to pick up ships, food, water, and supplies. You would think that now more than ever that was a necessity. Captain Anton boasted to me of hundreds of ships and thousands of worlds. That may have been a lie to impress me, but he certainly took time for the push-gun duel, drifting openly in space for hours as though he had no fear whatever of government interference. And Hansen said, moreover, that the pirates had appropriated the various hermit worlds as stopping-off places. There are hundreds of hermit worlds. If the pirates dealt with all of them, or even a good part of them, that also means a large organization.

"Now where do they get the food to support a large organization and at the same time mount fewer raids now than pirates did twenty-five years ago? The pirate crewman, Martin Maniu, spoke to me of wives and families. He was a vat-man, he said. Presumably he cultured yeast. Hansen had yeast foods on his asteroid and they weren't Venus yeast. I *know* the taste of Venus yeast.

"Put it all together. They grow their own food in small yeast farms distributed among asteroid caverns. They can get carbon dioxide directly from limestone rocks, and water and extra oxygen from the Jovian satellites. Machinery and power units may be imported from Sirius or obtained by an occasional raid. Raids will also supply them with more recruits, both men and women.

"What it amounts to is that Sirius is building an independent government against us. It's making use of discontented people to build a widespread society that will be difficult or impossible to crush if we wait too long. The leaders, the Captain Antons, are after power in the first place and they're perfectly willing to give half the Terrestrial Empire to Sirius if they themselves can keep the other half."

Conway shook his head. "That's an awfully big structure for the small foundation of fact you have. I doubt if we could convince the government. The Council of Science can act by itself only so far, you know. We don't have a fleet of our own, unfortunately."

"I know. That's exactly why we need more information. If, while it is still early in the game, we can find their major bases, capture their leaders, expose their Sirian connections—"

"Well?"

"Why, it's my opinion the movement would be done with. I'm convinced that the average 'man of the asteroids,' to use their own phrase, has no idea he's being made a Sirian puppet. He probably has a grievance against Earth. He may think he's had a raw deal, resent the fact that he couldn't find a job or advancement, that he wasn't getting along as well as he should have. He may have been attracted to what he thought would be a colorful life. All that, maybe. Still, that's a long way from saying he'd be willing to side with Earth's worst enemy. When he finds out that his leaders have been tricking him into doing just that, the pirate menace will fall apart."

Lucky halted his intense whispering as the technician approached, holding a flexible transparent tape with the computer's code prickings upon it.

"Say," he said, "are you sure these figures you gave me were right?"

Lucky said, "I'm sure. Why?"

The technician shook his head. "There's something wrong. The final co-ordinates put your rock inside of the forbidden zones. That's allowing for proper motion, too. I mean it can't be."

Lucky's eyebrows lifted sharply. The man was certainly right about the forbidden zones. No asteroids could possibly be found within them. Those zones represented portions of the asteroid belt in which asteroids, if they had existed, would have had times of revolution about the Sun that were an even fraction of Jupiter's twelve-year period of revolution. That would have meant that the asteroid and Jupiter would have continually approached, every few years, in the same portion of space. Jupiter's repeated pull would slowly move the asteroid out of that zone. In the two billion years since the planets had been formed Jupiter had cleared every asteroid out of the forbidden zone and that was that.

"Are you sure," Lucky said, "that your calculations are right?"

The technician shrugged as though to say, "I know my business." But aloud he only said, "We can check it by telescope. The thousand-incher is busy, but that's no good for close work anyway. We'll get one of the smaller ones. Will you follow me, please?"

The Observatory proper was almost like a shrine, with the various telescopes the altars. Men were absorbed in their work and did not pause to look up when the technician and the three Councilmen entered.

The technician led the way to one of the wings into which the huge, cavernous room was divided.

"Charlie," he said to a prematurely balding young man, "can you swing Bertha into action?"

"What for?" Charlie looked up from a series of photographic prints, star-speckled, over which he had been bending.

"I want to check the spot represented by these coordinates." He held out the computer film.

Charlie glanced at it and frowned. "What for? That's forbidden-zone territory."

"Would you focus the point anyway?" asked the technician. "It's Council of Science business."

"Oh? Yes, *sir*." He was suddenly far more pleasant. "It won't take long."

He closed a switch and a flexible diaphragm sucked inward high above, closing about the shaft of "Bertha," a hundred-twenty-inch telescope used for close work. The diaphragm made an air-tight seal, and above it Lucky could make out the smooth whir of the surface-lock opening. Bertha's large eye lifted upward, the diaphragm clinging, and was exposed to the heavens.

"Mostly," explained Charlie, "we use Bertha for photographic work. Ceres' rotation is too rapid for convenient optical observations. The point you're interested in is over the horizon, which is lucky."

He took his seat near the eyepiece, riding the telescope's shaft as though it were the stiff trunk of a giant elephant. The telescope angled and the young astronomer lifted high. Carefully he adjusted the focus.

He lifted out of his perch then and stepped down the rungs of a wall ladder. At the touch of his finger a partition directly below the telescope moved aside to show a black-lined pit. Into it a series of mirrors and lenses could focus and magnify the telescopic image.

There was only blackness.

Charlie said, "That's it." He used a meter stick as a point. "That little speck is Metis, which is a pretty big rock. It's twenty-five miles across, but it's millions of miles away. Here you have a few specks within a million miles of the point you're interested in, but they're to one side, outside the forbidden zone.

We've got the stars blanked out by phase polarization or they'd confuse everything."

"Thank you," said Lucky. He sounded stunned.

"Any time. Glad to help whenever I can."

They were in the elevator, headed downard, before Lucky spoke again. He said distantly, "It can't be."

"Why not?" said Henree. "Your figures were wrong."

"How could they be? I got to Ceres."

"You may have intended one figure and put down another by mistake, then made a correction by eye and forgot to correct the paper."

Lucky shook his head. "I couldn't have done that. I just don't— Wait. *Great Galaxy!*" He stared at them wildly.

"What's the matter, Lucky?"

"It works out! Space, it fits in! Look, I was wrong. It's not early in the game at all; it's darned late in the game. It may be too late. I've underestimated them again."

The elevator had reached the proper level. The door opened and Lucky was out with a rapid stride.

Conway ran after, seized his elbow, swung him about. "What are you talking about?"

"I'm going out there. Don't even think of stopping me. And if I don't come back, for Earth's sake, *force* the government to begin major preparations. Otherwise the pirates may be in control of the entire System within a year. Perhaps sooner."

"Why?" demanded Conway violently. "Because you couldn't find an asteroid?"

"Exactly," said Lucky.

# 10

## The Asteroid That Was

Bigman had brought Conway and Henree to Ceres
on Lucky's own ship, the *Shooting Starr,* and for that
Lucky was grateful. It meant he could go out into
space with it, feel its deck beneath his feet, hold its
controls in his hands.

The *Shooting Starr* was a two-man cruiser, built
this last year after Lucky's exploits among the farm
boys of Mars. Its appearance was as deceptive as
modern science could make it. It had almost the appearance of a space-yacht in its graceful lines, and
its extreme length was not more than twice that of
Hansen's little rowboat. No traveler in space, meeting
the *Shooting Starr,* would have estimated it to be
anything more than a rich man's plaything, speedy
perhaps but thin-skinned and unequal to hard knocks.
Certainly it would not have seemed the type of vessel
to trust in the dangerous reaches of the asteroid belt.

An investigation of the interior of the vessel might
have changed some of those notions, however. The
gleaming hyperatomic motors were the equal of those
on armored space-cruisers ten times the *Shooting*

*Starr's* weight. Its energy reserve was tremendous and the capacity of its hysteretic shield was sufficient to stop the largest projectile that could be put out against it by anything short of a dreadnought. Offensively its limited mass prevented it from being first-class, but weight for weight it could outfight any ship.

It was no wonder that Bigman capered with delight once he had entered the air-lock and thrown off his space-suit.

"Space," Bigman said, "I'm glad to get off that other tub. What do we do with it?"

"I'll have them send up a ship from Ceres to scoop it in."

Ceres was behind them, a hundred thousand miles away. In appearance it was about half the diameter of the Moon as seen from Earth.

Bigman said curiously, "How about letting me in on all this, Lucky? Why the sudden change of plans? I was heading out all by myself, the last I heard."

"There aren't any co-ordinates for you to head to," said Lucky. Grimly he told him the events of the last several hours.

Bigman whistled. "Then where are we going?"

"I'm not sure," said Lucky, "but we begin by aiming at the place where the hermit's rock ought to be now."

He studied the dials, and added, "And we leave here fast, too."

He *meant* fast. Acceleration on the *Shooting Starr* went high as velocity built up. Bigman and Lucky were pinned back to their diamagnetically cushioned chairs and the growing pressure spread evenly over their entire body surfaces. The oxygen concentration in the cabin was built up by the acceleration-sensitive air-purifier controls and allowed shallower breathing without oxygen starvation. The g-harness (g being the usual scientific symbol for acceleration) they both wore was light and did not hamper their movements, but under the stress of increasing velocity it stiffened and protected the bones, particularly the spine, from breaking. A nylotexmesh girdle kept the abdominal viscera from undue harm.

In every respect the cabin accessories had been designed by experts at the Council of Science to allow for twenty to thirty per cent greater acceleration on the *Shooting Starr* than on even the most advanced vessels of the fleet.

Even on this occasion the acceleration, though high, was less than half of that of which the ship was capable.

When velocity leveled off, the *Shooting Starr* was five million miles from Ceres, and, if Lucky or Bigman had been interested in looking for it, they would have found it to have become, in appearance, merely a speck of light, dimmer than many of the stars.

Bigman said, "Say, Lucky, I've been wanting to ask you. Do you have your glimmer shield?"

Lucky nodded and Bigman looked grieved.

"Well, you big dumb ox," the little fellow said, "why in space didn't you take it with you when you went out pirate-hunting then?"

"I did have it with me," said Lucky calmly. "I've had it with me since the day the Martians gave it to me."

As Lucky and Bigman (but no one else in the Galaxy) knew, the Martians to whom Lucky referred were not the farm boys and ranchers of Mars. They were rather a race of immaterial creatures who were the direct descendants of the ancient intelligences that once inhabited the surface of Mars in the ages before it had lost its oxygen and water. Excavating huge caverns below Mars' surface by destroying cubic miles of rock, converting the matter so destroyed into energy and storing that energy for future use, they now lived in comfortable isolation. Abandoning their material bodies and living as pure energy, their existence remained unsuspected by Mankind. Only Lucky Starr had penetrated their fastnesses and as the one souvenir of that eerie trip* he had obtained what Bigman called the "glimmer shield."

Bigman's annoyance increased. "Well, if you had it, why didn't you use it? What's wrong with you?"

"You have the wrong idea of the shield, Bigman. It won't do everything. It won't feed me and wipe my lips when I'm through."

"I've seen what it can do. It can do plenty."

"It can, in certain ways. It can soak up all types of energy."

"Like the energy of a blaster bolt. You're not going to kick about that, are you?"

"No, I admit I'd be immune to blasters. The shield would soak up potential energy, too, if the mass of a body weren't too great or too small. For instance, a knife or an ordinary bullet couldn't penetrate, though the bullet might knock me down. A good sledge hammer would swing right through the shield, though, and even if it didn't its momentum would crush me. And what's more, molecules of air can go

*See David Starr, Space Ranger

through the shield as if it weren't there because they're too small to be handled. I'm telling you this so that you'll understand that if I were wearing the shield and Dingo had broken my face plate when we were both tangled up in space, I would have died anyway. The shield wouldn't have prevented the air in my suit from scattering away in a split second."

"If you had used it in the first place, Lucky, you wouldn't have had any trouble. Don't I remember when you used it on Mars?" Bigman chuckled at the reminiscence. "It glimmered all over you, smoky-like, only luminous, so you could just be seen in a haze. All except your face anyway. That was just a sheet of white light."

"Yes," said Lucky dryly, "I would have scared them. They would have hit at me with blasters and I wouldn't have been hurt. So they would have all high-tailed it off the *Atlas,* gone off about ten miles, and blasted the ship. I would have been stone dead. Don't forget that the shield is only a shield. It doesn't give me any offensive powers whatever."

"Aren't you ever going to use it again?" asked Bigman.

"When it's necessary. Not till then. If I use it too much, the effect would be lost. Its weaknesses would be found out and I would be just a target for anyone I came up against."

Lucky studied the instruments. Calmly he said, "Ready for acceleration again."

Bigman said, "Hey——"

Then, as he was pushed back into his seat, he found himself fighting for breath and could say nothing more. The redness was rising to his eyes and he could feel the skin drawing backward as though it were trying to peel off his bones.

This time the *Shooting Starr*'s acceleration was on full.

It lasted fifteen minutes. Toward the end Bigman was scarcely conscious. Then it relaxed and life crept back.

Lucky was shaking his head and panting for breath.

Bigman said, "Hey, that wasn't funny."

"I know," said Lucky.

"What's the idea? Weren't we going fast enough?"

"Not quite. But it's all right now. We've shaken them."

"Shaken whom?"

"Whoever was following us. We were being followed, Bigman, from the minute you stepped foot on the deck of the old Shooter. Look at the Ergometer."

Bigman did so. The Ergometer resembled the one on the *Atlas* in name only. The one on the *Atlas* had been a primitive model designed to pick up motor radiation for the purpose of releasing the lifeboats. That had been its only purpose. The Ergometer on the *Shooting Starr* could pick up the radiation pattern of a hyperatomic motor on ships no larger than an ordinary lifeboat and do it at a distance of better than two million miles.

Even now the inked line on the graphed paper jiggled very faintly, but periodically.

"That isn't anything," said Bigman.

"It was, a while ago. Look for yourself." Lucky unreeled the cylinder of paper that had already passed the needle. The jigglings grew deeper, more characteristic. "See that, Bigman?"

"It could be any ship. It could be a Ceres freighter."

"No. For one thing, it tried to follow us and did a good job of it, too, which means it had a pretty good Ergometer of its own. Besides that, did you ever see an energy pattern like this?"

"Not exactly like this, Lucky."

"I did, you see, in the case of the ship that boarded the *Atlas*. This Ergometer does a much better job of pattern analysis, but the resemblance is definite. The motor of the ship that's following us is of Sirian design."

"You mean it's Anton's ship."

"That or a similar one. It doesn't matter. We've lost them."

"At the moment," said Lucky, "we're right where the hermit's rock should be, plus or minus, say, a hundred thousand miles."

"Nothing's here," said Bigman.

"That's right. The gravitics register no asteroidal mass anywhere near us. We're in what the astronomers call a forbidden zone."

"Uh-huh," said Bigman wisely, "I see."

Lucky smiled. There was nothing to see. A forbidden zone in the asteroid belt looked no different from a portion of the belt that was thickly strewn with rocks, at least not to the naked eye. Unless an asteroid happened to be within a hundred miles or so, the view was the same. Stars or things that looked like stars filled the heavens. If some of them were asteroids and not stars, there was no way of telling the difference short of watching intently for several hours to see which "stars" changed relative postion, or using a telescope to begin with.

Bigman said, "Well, what do we do?"

"Look around the neighborhood. It may take us a few days."

The path of the *Shooting Starr* grew erratic. It headed outward from the Sun, away from the forbidden zone and into the nearest constellation of asteroids. The gravitics jumped their needles at the pull of distant mass.

Tiny world after tiny world slid into the field of the visiplate, was allowed to remain there while it rotated, and was then permitted to slip out. The *Shooting Starr*'s velocity had decelerated to a relative crawl, but the miles still passed by the hundreds of thousands and into the millions. The hours passed. A dozen asteroids came and went.

"You better eat," said Bigman.

But Lucky contented himself with sandwiches and catnaps while he and Bigman watched visiplate, gravitics and Ergometer in turn.

Then, with an asteroid in view, Lucky said in a strained voice, "I'm going down."

Bigman was caught by surprise. "Is that the asteroid?" He looked at its angularity. "Do you recognize it?"

"I think I do, Bigman. In any case, it's going to be investigated."

It took half an hour to manipulate the ship into the asteroid's shadow.

"Keep it here," Lucky said. "Someone's got to stay with the ship and you're the one. Don't forget it. It can be detected, but if it's in the shadow, with the lights out and the motors at minimum, it will make it as hard as possible for them. According to the Ergometer, there's no ship in space near us now. Right?"

"Right!"

"The most important thing to remember is this: Don't come down after me for any reason. When I'm through, I'll come up to you. If I'm not back in twelve hours and haven't called, either, back you go to Ceres with a report, after taking photographs of this asteroid at every angle."

Bigman's face grew sullenly stubborn. "No."

"This is the report," said Lucky calmly. He withdrew a personal capsule from an inner pocket. "This capsule is keyed to Dr. Conway. He's the only one who can open it. He's got to get the information, regardless of me. Do you understand?"

"What's in it?" asked Bigman, making no move to take it.

"Just theories, I'm afraid. I've told no one of them, because I've come out here to try to get facts to back them up. If I can't make it, the theories, at least, must get through. Conway may believe them and he may get the government to act upon them."

"I won't do it," said Bigman. "I won't leave you."

"Bigman, if I can't trust you to do what's right regardless of yourself and myself, you won't be much use to me after this if I come through safely."

Bigman held out his hand. The personal capsule was dropped into it.

"All right," he said.

Lucky dropped through vacuum to the asteroid's surface, hastening the drop by use of the suit's push-gun. He knew the asteroid to be about the right size. It was roughly the shape he remembered it to be. It was jagged enough and the sunlit portion looked the right color. All that, however, might have held true for any asteroid.

But there was the other item. That was not likely to be duplicated very often.

From his waist pouch he took out a small instrument that looked like a compass. Actually it was a pocket radar unit. Its enclosed emission source could put out radio short waves of almost any range. Certain octaves could be partially reflected by rock and partially transmitted through reasonable distances.

In the presence of a thick layer of rock the reflection of radiation activated a needle on the dial. In the presence of a thin layer of rock, as, for instance, on a surface under which lay a cave or hollow, some radiation was reflected, but some penetrated into the hollow and was reflected from the further wall. In this way a double reflection occurred, one component of which was much weaker than the second. In response to such a double reflection the needle responded with a characteristic double quiver.

Lucky watched the instrument as he leaped easily over the stony peaks. The needle's smooth pulsing gained a quiver, and then a distinct subsidiary movement. Lucky's heart bounded. The asteroid was hollow. Find where the subsidiary movements were strongest and there the hollow would be nearest the surface. There would be the air-lock.

For a few moments all of Lucky's faculties were concentrated on the needle. He was unaware of the magnetic cable snaking its way toward him from the near horizon.

He was unaware of it until it snapped about him in coil after coil, clinging close, its momentum tossing his nearly weightless body first clear of the asteroid and then down to the rock, where he lay helpless.

# 11

## At Close Quarters

Three lights came over the horizon and toward the prostrate Lucky. In the darkness of the asteroid's night he could not see the figures that accompanied the lights.

Then there was a voice in his ear and the voice was the well-known hoarseness of the pirate, Dingo. It said, "Don't call your pal upstairs. I've got a jigger here that can pick up your carrier wave. If you try to, I'll blast you out of your suit right now, nark!"

He spat out the final word; the contemptuous term of all lawbreakers for those they considered to be spies of the law-enforcement agencies.

Lucky kept silent. From the moment he had first felt the tremor of his suit under the lash of the magnetic cable he knew that he had fallen into a trap. To call Bigman before he knew more about the nature of the trap would have been putting the *Shooting Starr* into danger, and that without helping himself.

Dingo stood over him, a foot on either side. In the light of one of the flashes Lucky caught a quick glimpse of Dingo's face-plate and of the stubby goggles that covered his eyes. Lucky knew those to be infrared translators, capable of converting ordinary heat radiation into visible light. Even without flashes and in the asteroid's dark night they had been able to watch him by the energy of his own heaters.

Dingo said, "What's the matter, nark? Scared?"

He lifted a bulky leg with its bulkier metal swathing and brought his heel down sharply in the direction of Lucky's face-plate. Lucky turned his head swiftly away to let the blow fall on the sturdier metal of the helmet, but Dingo's heel stopped midway. He laughed whoopingly.

"You won't get it that easy, nark," he said.

His voice changed as he spoke to the other two pirates. "Hop over the jag and get the air-lock open."

For a moment they hesitated. One of them said, "But, Dingo, the captain said you were too——"

Dingo said, "Get going, or maybe I'll start with him and finish with you."

In the face of the threat the two hopped away. Dingo said to Lucky, "Now suppose we get you to the air-lock."

He was still holding the butt end of the magnetic cable. With a flick at the switch he turned off its current and momentarily demagnetized it. He stepped away and pulled it sharply toward himself. Lucky dragged along the rocky floor of the asteroid, bounced upward, and rolled partly out of the cable. Dingo touched the switch again and the remaining coils suddenly clung and held.

Dingo flicked the whip upward. Lucky traveled with it, while Dingo maneuvered skillfully to maintain his own balance. Lucky hovered in space and Dingo walked with him as though he were a child's balloon at the end of a string.

The lights of the other two were visible again after five minutes. They were shining into a patch of darkness of which regular boundaries were proof enough that it was an open air-lock.

Dingo called, "Watch out! I've got a package to deliver."

He demagnetized the cable again, and flicked it downward, rising six inches into the air as he did so. Lucky rotated rapidly, spinning completely out of the cable.

Dingo leaped upward and caught him. With the skill of a man long used to weightlessness, he avoided Lucky's attempts to break his hold, and hurled him in the direction of the air-lock. He broke his own backward tumble by a quick double spurt of his suit's push-gun and righted himself in time to see Lucky enter the air-lock cleanly.

What followed was clearly visible in the light of the pirates' flashes. Caught in the pseudo-grav field that existed within the air-lock, Lucky was hurled suddenly downward, hitting the rocky floor with a clatter and force that knocked the breath out of him. Dingo's braying laughter filled his helmet.

The outer door closed, the inner opened. Lucky got to his feet, actually thankful for the normality of gravity.

"Get in, nark." Dingo was holding a blaster.

Lucky paused as he entered the asteroid's interior. His eyes shifted quickly from side to side while the frost gathered at the rims of his face-plate. What he saw was not the soft-lit library of the hermit, Hansen, but a tremendously long hallway, the roof of which was supported by a series of pillars. He could not see to the other end. Openings to rooms pierced the wall of the corridors regularly. Men hurried to and fro and there was the smell of ozone and machine oil in the air. In the distance he could hear the characteristic drum-drum of what must have been gigantic hyper-atomic motors.

It was quite obvious that this was no hermit's cell, but a large industrial plant, *inside an asteroid*.

Lucky bit his lower lip thoughtfully and wondered despondently if all this information would die with him now.

Dingo said, "In there, nark. Get in there."

It was a storeroom he indicated, its shelves and bins well filled, but empty of human beings other than themselves.

"Say, Dingo," said one of the pirates nervously, "why are we showing him all this? I don't think—"

"Then don't talk," said Dingo, and laughed. "Don't worry, he won't tell anyone about anything he sees. I guarantee that. Meanwhile I have a little something to finish with him. Get that suit off him."

He was removing his own suit as he spoke. He stepped out, monstrously bulky. One hand rubbed slowly over the hairy back of the other. He was savoring the moment.

Lucky said firmly, "Captain Anton never gave you orders to kill me. You're trying to finish a private feud and it will only get you into trouble. I'm a valuable man to the captain and he knows it."

Dingo sat down on the edge of a bin of small metal objects, with a grin on his face. "To listen to you, nark, you'd think you had a case. But you didn't fool us, not for one minute. When we left you on the rock with the hermit, what do you think we did? We *watched*. Captain Anton's no fool. He sent me back. He said, 'Watch that rock and report back.' I saw the hermit's dinghy leave. I could have blasted you out of space then, but the order was to follow.

"I stayed off Ceres for a day and a half and spotted the hermit's dinghy hitting out for space again. I waited some more. Then I caught this other ship coming out to meet it. The man off the dinghy got on to the other ship and I followed you when you took off."

Lucky could not help smiling. "Tried to follow, you mean."

Dingo's face turned a blotchy red. He spat out, "All right. You were faster. Your kind is good at running. What of it? I didn't have to chase you. I just came here and waited. I knew where you were heading. I've got you, haven't I?"

Lucky said, "All right, but what have you got? I was unarmed on the hermit's rock. I didn't have any weapons, while the hermit had a blaster. I had to do what he said. He wanted to get back to Ceres and he forced me along so he could claim he was being kidnapped if the men of the asteroids stopped him. You admit yourself that I got off Ceres as fast as I could and tried to get back here."

"In a nice, shiny government ship?"

"I stole it. So? It just means that you've got another ship for your fleet. And a good one."

Dingo looked at the other pirates. "Doesn't he throw the comet-dust, though?"

Lucky said, "I warn you again. The captain will take anything that happens to me out on you."

"No he won't," snarled Dingo, "because he knows who you are and so do I, Mr. David Lucky Starr. Come on, move out into the middle of the room."

Dingo rose. He said to his two companions, "Get those bins out of the way. Pull them over to one side."

They looked at his staring, blood-congested face once and did as he said. Dingo's bulbously thickset body was slightly stooped, his head sank down into his bulging shoulders, and his thick, somewhat bandy, legs planted themselves firmly. The scar on his upper lip was a vivid white.

He said, "There are easy ways of finishing you and there are nice ways. I don't like a nark and I especially don't like a nark who fouls me in a push-gun fight. So before I finish you, I'm breaking you into little pieces."

Lucky, looking tall and spindly in comparison with the other, said, "Are you man enough to take care of me alone, Dingo, or will your two friends help you?"

"I don't need help, pretty boy." He laughed nastily. "But if you try to run, they'll stop you, and if you keep on trying to run, they've got neuronic whips that will *really* stop you." He raised his voice. "And use them, you two, if you have to."

Lucky waited for the other to make his move. He knew that the one most nearly fatal tactic would be to try to mix it up at close quarters. Let the pirate enclose his chest in the hug of those enormous arms and broken ribs would be the nearly certain result.

Dingo, right fist drawn back, ran forward. Lucky stood his ground as long as he dared, then stepped

quickly to his right, seized his opponent's extended left
arm, pulled backward, taking advantage of the other's
forward momentum, and caught the other's ankle
against his foot.

Dingo went sprawling forward and down heavily.
He was up immediately, however, one cheek scraped
and little lights of madness dancing in his eyes.

He thundered toward Lucky, who retired nimbly
toward one of the bins lining the wall.

Lucky seized the ends of the bin and swung his legs
up and out. Dingo caught them in his chest, halted
momentarily. Lucky whirled out of the way and was
free in the center of the room again.

One of the pirates called out, "Hey, Dingo, let's stop
fooling around."

Dingo panted, "I'll kill him, I'll kill him."

But he was more cautious now. His little eyes were
nearly buried in the fat and gristle that surrounded his
eyeballs. He crept forward, watching Lucky, waiting
for the moment he might strike.

Lucky said, "What's the matter, Dingo? Afraid of
me? You get afraid very quick for such a big talker."

As Lucky expected, Dingo roared incoherently and
dashed heavily and directly at him. Lucky had no
trouble in evading the bull rush. The side of his hand
came sharply and swiftly down on the back of Dingo's
neck.

Lucky had seen any number of men knocked un-
conscious by that particular blow; he had seen more
than one killed. But Dingo merely staggered. He
shook it off and turned, snarling.

He walked flat-footedly toward the dancing Lucky.
Lucky lashed out with his fist, which landed sharply

on Dingo's scraped cheek bone. Blood flowed, but Dingo did not so much as attempt to block the blow, nor did he blink when it landed.

Lucky squirmed away and struck sharply twice more at the pirate. Dingo paid no attention. He came forward, always forward.

Suddenly, unexpectedly, he went down, apparently as a man who had stumbled. But his arms shot out as he fell and one hand closed about Lucky's right ankle. Lucky went down too.

"I've got you now," whispered Dingo.

He reached up to catch Lucky's waist and in a moment, fast-locked, they were rolling across the floor.

Lucky felt the growing, enclosing pressure and pain washed inward like an advancing flame. Dingo's fetid panting was in his ear.

Lucky's right arm was free, but his left was enclosed in the numbing vise of the other's grip about his chest. With the last of his fading strength, Lucky brought his right fist up. The blow traveled no more than four inches, catching the point where Dingo's chin met his neck with a force that sent stabs of pain the length of Lucky's arm.

Dingo's grip loosened for a moment and Lucky, writhing, flung himself out of the deadly embrace and onto his feet.

Dingo got up more slowly. His eyes were glassy, and fresh blood was trickling out the corner of his mouth.

He muttered thickly, "The whip! The whip!"

Unexpectedly he turned upon one of the pirates who had been standing there a frozen onlooker. He wrested the weapon from the other's hand and sent him sprawling.

Lucky tried to duck, but the neuronic whip was up and flashing. It caught his right side and stimulated the nerves of the area it struck into a bath of pain. Lucky's body stiffened and went down again.

For a moment his senses recorded only confusion, and with what consciousness he possessed he expected death to be a second off. Dimly he heard a pirate's voice.

"Look, Dingo, the captain said to make it look like an accident. He's a Council of Science man and . . ."

It was all Lucky heard.

When he swam back to consciousness with an excruciating tingle of pins and needles down the length of his side, he found himself in a space-suit again. They were just about to put on his helmet. Dingo, lips puffed, cheek and jaw bruised, watched malignantly.

There was a voice in the doorway. A man was entering hurriedly, full of talk.

Lucky heard him say, "—for Post 247. It's getting so *I* can't keep track of all the requisitions. I can't even keep our own orbit straight enough to keep up the co-ordinate corrections of——"

The voice flickered out. Lucky twisted his head and caught sight of a small man with spectacles and gray hair. He was just inside the doorway, looking with mingled astonishment and disbelief at the disorder that met his eyes.

"Get out," roared Dingo.

"But I've got to have a requisition——"

"Later!"

The little man left and the helmet was fitted over Lucky's head.

They took him out again, through the air-lock, to a surface which was now in the feeble blaze of the distant Sun. A catapult waited on a relatively flat table of rock. Its function was no mystery to Lucky. An automatic winch was drawing back a large metal lever which bent more and more slowly till its original slant had strained back into a complete horizontal at the tip. Light straps were attached to the bent lever and then buckled about Lucky's waist.

"Lie still," said Dingo. His voice was dim and scratchy in Lucky's ear. There was something wrong with the helmet receiver, Lucky realized. "You're just wasting your oxygen. Just to make you feel better, we're sending ships up to blast your friend down before he can pick up speed, if he feels like running."

An instant after that Lucky felt the sharp tingling vibration of the lever as it was released. It sprang elastically back into its original position with terrific force. The buckles about him parted smoothly and he was cast off at a speed of a mile a minute or better, with no gravitational field to slow him. There was one glimpse of the asteroid with the pirates looking up at him. The whole was shrinking rapidly even as he watched.

He inspected his suit. He already knew that his helmet radio had been maltreated. Sure enough, the sensitivity knob hung loose. It meant his voice could penetrate no more than a few miles of space. They had left him his space-suit's push-gun. He tried it but nothing happened. Its gas stores had been drained.

He was quite helpless. There were only the contents of one oxygen cylinder between himself and a slow, unpleasant death.

# 12

## Ship Versus Ship

With a clammy constriction of his chest Lucky surveyed the situation. He thought he could guess the pirates' plans. On the one hand, they wished to get rid of him, since he obviously knew far too much. On the other hand, they must want him to be found dead in such a way that the Council of Science would be unable to prove conclusively that his death was by pirate violence.

Once before, pirates had made the mistake of killing an agent of the Council and the resultant fury had been crushing. They would be more cautious this time.

He thought, They'll rush the *Shooting Starr*, blanket it with interference to keep Bigman from sending out a call for help. Then they can use a cannon blast on its hull. It would make a good imitation of a meteorite collision. They can make that look better by sending their own engineers on board to hocus the shield activators. It would look as though a defect in the mechanism had prevented the shield from going up as the meteorite approached.

They would know his own course through space, Lucky knew. There would be nothing to deflect him from whatever his original angles of flight had been. Later, with him safely dead, they would pick him up and send him whirling in an orbit about the broken *Shooting Starr*. The discoverers (and perhaps one of their own ships would send in an anonymous report of the find) would reach an obvious conclusion. Bigman at the controls, maneuvering to the last, killed at his post. Lucky, on the other hand, scrambling into a suit, damaging the external sensitivity knob of the suit's radio in the excitement. He would have been unable to call for help. He would have expended his push-gun's gas in a desperate and futile attempt to find a place of safety. And he would have died.

It would not work. Neither Conway nor Henree could possibly believe that Lucky would be concerned only with his own safety while Bigman stuck loyally at the controls. But then, the failure of the scheme would be small satisfaction to a dead Lucky Starr. Worse yet, it would not only be Lucky Starr who would die, but all the information now locked in Lucky Starr's head.

For a moment he was sick with outrage at himself that he had not forced all his suspicions on Conway and Henree before leaving, that he had waited till he boarded the *Shooting Starr* before preparing the personal capsule. Then he gained control of himself. No one would have believed him without facts.

For that very reason he would have to get back. Have to!

But how? What good was "have to" when one was

alone and helpless in space with a few hours' worth of oxygen and nothing else?

Oxygen!

Lucky thought, There's my oxygen. Anyone but Dingo would have drained his cylinder of all but dregs, to let death come quickly. But if Lucky knew Dingo, the pirate had sent him on his way with a loaded cylinder simply to prolong the agony.

Good! Then he would reverse that. He would use the oxygen otherwise. And if he failed, death would come the sooner, despite Dingo.

Only he must not fail.

The asteroid had been crossing his line of vision periodically as he spun in space. First, it was a shrinking rock, its sunlit highlights slanting jaggedly across the blackness of space. Then it had been a bright star and a single line of light. The brightness was fading quickly now. Once the asteroid became dim enough to be simply one more in the myriad of stars, it was all over. Not many minutes were left before that would be the case.

His clumsy, metal-covered fingers were already fumbling with the flexible tube that led from the air inlet just under the face-plate to the oxygen cylinder in back. He twisted strenuously at the bolt that held the air tube tightly fixed to the cylinder.

It gave. He paused to fill his helmet and suit with oxygen. Ordinarily oxygen leaked slowly in from the cylinders at about the rate it was used up by human lungs. The carbon dioxide and water formed as the result of respiration were mostly absorbed by the chemicals contained in the valved canisters affixed to the inner surface of the suit's chest plates. The result was the oxygen was kept at a pressure one fifth that of Earth's atmosphere. This was exactly right, since four fifths of Earth's atmosphere is nitrogen anyway, which is useless for breathing.

However, this left room for higher concentrations, up to somewhat more than normal atmospheric pressure, before there was danger of toxic effects. Lucky let the oxygen pour into his suit.

Then, having done so, he closed the valve under his face-plate entirely and removed the cylinder.

The cylinder was itself a sort of push-gun. It was an unusual push-gun, to be sure. For a person marooned in space to use the precious oxygen that stood between himself and death as motive power, to blow it into space, meant desperation. Or else, a firm resolution.

Lucky cracked the reducing valve and let a blast of oxygen issue out. There was no line of crystals this time. Oxygen, unlike carbon dioxide, froze at very low temperatures indeed and before it could lose sufficient heat to freeze, it had diffused out into space. Gas or solid, however, Newton's third law of motion still held. As the gas pushed out one way, Lucky was pushed in the opposite direction by a natural counter-push.

His spinning slowed. Carefully he allowed the asteroid to come into full view before stopping the spin completely.

He was still receding from the rock. It was no longer particularly brighter than the neighboring stars. Conceivably he had already mistaken his target, but he closed his mind against that uncertainty.

He fixed his eyes firmly on the spot of light he assumed to be the asteroid and let the cylinder blast in the opposite direction. He wondered if he would have enough to reverse the direction of his travel. There was no way of telling at the moment.

In any case, he would have to save some gas. He would need it to maneuver about the asteroid, get on its night side, find Bigman and the ship, unless . . .

Unless the ship had already been driven away, or destroyed, by the pirates.

It seemed to Lucky that the vibration of his hands, due to the escaping oxygen, was lessening. Either the cylinder was running low, or its temperature was dropping. He was holding it away from his suit so it was no longer absorbing heat from it. It was from the suit that oxygen cylinders gained enough heat to be breathable, and the carbon dioxide cylinders of the push-guns gained enough heat to keep their contents gaseous. In the vacuum of space heat could be lost only by radiation, a slow process, but, even so, the oxygen cylinder had had time to drop in temperature.

He encircled the cylinder in his arms, hugged it to his chest, and waited.

It seemed hours, but only fifteen minutes passed before it seemed to him that the asteroid was growing brighter. Was he approaching the rock again? Or was it imagination? Another fifteen minutes passed and it was distinctly brighter. Lucky felt a deep gratitude to the chance that had shot him out on the sunlit side of the rock so that he could see it plainly as a target.

It was getting harder to breathe. There was no question of carbon dioxide asphyxiation. That gas was removed as it was formed. Still, each breath also removed a small fraction of his precious oxygen. He tried to breathe shallowly, close his eyes, rest. After all, he could do nothing more until he had reached and passed the asteroid. There on the night side, Bigman might still be waiting.

Then, if he could get close enough to Bigman, if he could call him on his limping radio before he passed out, there might yet be a chance.

The hours had passed slowly and torturously for Bigman. He longed to descend, but dared not. He reasoned with himself that, if the enemy existed, he would have shown himself by now. Then he argued it out bitterly and came to the conclusion that the very silence and motionlessness of space meant a trap, and that Lucky was caught.

He put Lucky's personal capsule before him and wondered about its contents. If only there were some way of bursting it, of reading the thin roll of microfilm within. If he could do that, he could radio it to Ceres, get it off his hands, and be free to go slamming down to the rock. He would blast them all, drag Lucky out of whatever mess he was in.

No! In the first place he dared not use the sub-etherics. True, the pirates could not break the code, but they would detect the carrier wave and he had been instructed not to give away the location of the ship.

Besides, what was the use of thinking of breaking into a personal capsule. A solar furnace could melt and destroy it, an atom blast could disintegrate it, but nothing could open it and leave its message intact except the living touch of the person for whom it had been "personalized." That was that.

More than half of the twelve-hour period had passed when the gravitics gave their entirely distinctive warning.

Bigman roused himself out of his frustrated reverie and stared with shocked surprise at the Ergometer. The pulsations of several ships were blending themselves into complicated curves that melted snakelike from one configuration to another.

The *Shooting Starr*'s shield, which had been glimmering routinely at a strength sufficient to ward off casual "debris" (the usual space term for wandering meteorites an inch or less in diameter) stiffened to maximum. Bigman heard the soft purr of the power output grow strident. One by one, he let the short-range visiplates glow into life, bank on bank of them.

His mind churned. The ships were rising from the asteroid, since none could be detected further away. Lucky must be caught, then; dead, probably. He didn't care now how many ships came at him. He would get them all, every single one of them.

He sobered. The first Sun glint had caught in one of the visiplates. He maneuvered the cross hairs and centered them. He then depressed something that looked like a piano key and, caught in an invisible burst of energy, the pirate ship glowed.

The glow was not due to any action upon its hull, but was rather the result of the energy absorption of the enemy screen. It glowed brightly and more brightly still. Then it dimmed as the enemy turned tail and put distance between them.

A second ship and a third were in view. A projectile was making its way toward the *Shooting Starr*. In the vacuum of space there was no flash, no sound, but the Sun caught it and it was a little sparking spot of light. It became a little circle in the visiplate, then a larger one, until finally it moved out of the plate's field.

Bigman might have dodged, flashed the Shooter out of the way, but he thought, Let it hit. He wanted them to see what they were playing with. The Shooter might look like a rich man's toy, but they weren't going to put it out of action with a few slingshooters.

The projectile stuck and slogged to a halt against the *Shooting Starr*'s hysteretic shields, which, Bigman knew, must have flashed momentarily into brilliance. The ship itself moved smoothly, absorbing the momentum that had leaked past the shield.

"Let's return that," Bigman muttered. The *Shooting Starr* carried no projectiles, explosive or otherwise, but its store of energy projectors was varied and powerful.

His hand was hovering over the blaster controls when he saw in one of the visiplates something that brought a scowl to his small, determined face, something that looked like a man in a space-suit.

It was strange that the space-ship was more vulnerable to a man in a space-suit than to the best weapons of another ship. An enemy ship could be easily detected by gravitics at a distance of miles and by Ergometers at a distance of thousands of miles. A single man in a space-suit could only be detected by a gravitic at a hundred yards and by an Ergometer not at all.

Again, a hysteretic shield worked the more effectively the greater the velocity of the projectile. Huge lumps of metal tearing at miles per second could be stopped cold. One man, however, drifting along at ten miles an hour was not even aware of the existence of the shield except for a tiny warming of his suit.

Let a dozen men creep toward a ship at once and only great skill could bring them all down. If two or three penetrated and succeeded in blasting open the air-lock with hand weapons, the ship they attacked was seriously crippled.

And now Bigman caught the little speck that could only mean the advance guard of such a suicide squadron. He brought one of the secondaries to bear. The single figure was centered and Bigman was ready to fire when his radio receiver sounded.

For a moment he was startled. The pirates had attacked without warning and had not tried to communicate, to call for surrender, to offer terms, anything. What now?

He hesitated and the sounding became a word, repeated twice, "Bigman . . . Bigman . . . Bigman . . ."

Bigman jumped from his seat, ignoring the suited man, the battle, everything. "Lucky! Is that you?"

"I'm near the ship . . . Space-suit . . . Air . . . nearly gone."

"Great Galaxy!" Bigman, white-faced, maneuvered the *Shooting Starr* nearer the figure in space, the figure whom he had nearly destroyed.

Bigman watched over Lucky, who, helmet off, was still gulping air. "You'd better get some rest, Lucky."

"Later," said Lucky. He climbed out of his suit. "Have they attacked yet?"

Bigman nodded. "It doesn't matter. They're just breaking their teeth on the old Shooter."

"They've got stronger teeth than any they've shown," said Lucky. "We've got to get away and fast. They'll be bringing out their heavy craft, and even *our* energy stores won't last forever."

"Where are they going to get heavy craft from?"

"That's a major pirate base down there! *The* major base, perhaps."

"You mean it *isn't* the hermit's rock?"

"I mean we've got to get away."

He took the controls, face still pale from his ordeal. For the first time the rock below them moved from its position on the screens. Even during the attack Bigman had heeded Lucky's parting order to stay put for twelve hours.

The rock grew larger.

Bigman protested. "If we've got to get away, why are we landing?"

"We're not landing." Lucky watched the screen intently, while one hand set the controls of the ship's heavy blaster. Deliberately he widened and softened the focus of the blaster till it could cover a broad area indeed, but at an energy intensity reduced to little more than that of an ordinary heat ray.

He waited, for reasons that the wondering Bigman could not divine, and then fired. There was a startling blazing brightness on the asteroid's surface which subsided almost instantly into a glowing redness that in a further minute or so blackened out.

"Now let's go," said Lucky, and, as new ships spiraled up from the pirate base, acceleration took hold.

Half an hour later, with asteroid gone and any pursuing ships safely lost, he said, "Get Ceres, I want to speak to Conway."

"Okay, Lucky. And listen, I've got the co-ordinates of the asteroid. Shall I send them along? We can send a fleet back and—"

"It won't do any good," said Lucky, "and it isn't necessary."

Bigman's eyes widened. "You don't mean you destroyed the rock with that blaster bolt?"

"Of course not. I hardly touched it," said Lucky. "Have you got Ceres?"

"I'm having trouble," said Bigman pettishly. He knew Lucky was in one of his tight-mouthed moods and would give no information. "Wait, here it is, but, hey— They're broadcasting a general alarm!"

There was no need to explain that. The call was strident and uncoded. "General call to all fleet units outside Mars. Ceres under attack by enemy force, presumed pirates. . . . General call to all fleet units . . ."

Bigman said, "Great Galaxy!"

Lucky said tightly, "They stay one step ahead of us, no matter what we do. We've got to get back! Quickly!"

# 13

## Raid!

The ships came swarming out of space in perfect co-ordination. An entire wing struck directly at the Observatory. In response to this, almost inevitably, the defending forces on Ceres concentrated their power at that point.

The attack was not pressed full-force. Ship after ship dived downward to launch energy beams at an obviously impregnable shield. None took the risky step of trying to blast the underground power plants, the location of which they must have known. Government ships took to space and ground batteries opened up. In the end two pirate ships were destroyed when their shields broke down and they flared into glowing vapor. Another one, its energy reserves down to a trickle, was almost captured in the eventual pursuit. It was blown up at the last moment, probably by its own crew.

Even during the attack some of the defenders suspected it to be a feint. Later, of course, they knew that for a fact. While the Observatory was engaged, three ships landed on the asteroid a hundred miles away. Pirates disembarked and with hand weapons and portable blasting cannon attacked the residential air-locks from flitting "space-sleds."

The locks were blasted open and space-suited pirates swarmed down the corridors from which air emptied. The upper reaches of the corridors were factories and offices, the occupants of which had evacuated at the first alarm. Their place was taken by space-suited members of the local militia who fought bravely, but were no match for the professionals of the pirate fleet.

In the lower depths, in the peaceful apartments of Ceres, the noise of blasting battle sounded. Calls for help were sent out. Then, almost as suddenly as they came, the pirates retreated.

When they left, the men of Ceres counted their casualties. Fifteen Cereans were dead and many more hurt in one way or another, as against the bodies of five pirates. Damage to property was very high.

"And one man," Conway explained furiously to Lucky when the latter arrived, "is missing. Only he's not on the list of inhabitants and we've been able to keep his name out of the news reports."

Lucky found Ceres the focus of almost hysterical excitement now that the raid was over. It had been the first attack on an important Terrestrial center by any enemy in a generation. He had had to pass three inspections before being allowed to land.

He sat in the Council office with Conway and Henree and said bitterly, "So Hansen is gone! That's what it boils down to."

"I'll say this for the old hermit," said Henree. "He

had guts. When the pirates penetrated, he insisted on getting into a suit, grabbing up a blaster, and going up there with the militia."

"We weren't short on militia," said Lucky. "If he had stayed down here, he would have done us a much greater service. How is it you didn't stop him? Under the circumstances was he a person to be allowed to do such a thing?" Lucky Starr's usually even voice contained a repressed anger.

Conway said patiently, "We weren't with him. The guard we left in charge had to report for militia duty. Hansen insisted on joining him and the guard decided he could do both duties at once that way; fight the pirates and guard the hermit."

"But he didn't guard the hermit."

"Under the circumstances he can scarcely be blamed. The guard saw Hansen last charging a pirate. Next thing he knew there was no one in sight and the pirates were retreating. Hansen's body hasn't been recovered. The pirates must have him alive or dead."

"So they must," said Lucky. "Now let me tell you something. Let me tell you exactly what a bad mistake this was. I'm certain that the whole attack on Ceres was arranged simply to capture Hansen."

Henree reached for his pipe. "You know, Hector," he said to Conway, "I'm almost tempted to go along with Lucky on that. The attack on the Observatory was a miserable one, an obvious false alarm to draw off our defenses. Getting Hansen was the only thing they did accomplish."

Conway snorted. "One possible information leak like the hermit isn't worth risking thirty ships."

"That's the whole point," said Lucky vehemently.

"Right now, it may be. I told you about the asteroid I was on, the kind of industrial plant it must have been. Suppose they're almost at the point where they're ready to make the big push? Suppose Hansen knows the exact date for when the push is scheduled? Suppose he knows the exact method?"

"Then why hasn't he told us?" demanded Conway.

"Maybe," said Henree, "he's waiting to use it as material with which to buy his own immunity. We never did have a chance really to discuss that question with him. You've got to admit, Hector, that if he had that kind of key information, any number of ships would have been worth the risk. And you've got to admit Lucky is probably right about their being ready for the big push."

Lucky looked sharply from one to the other. "Why do you say that, Uncle Gus? What happened?"

"Tell him, Hector," said Henree.

"Why tell him anything," growled Conway. "I'm tired of his one-man trips. He'll be wanting to go to Ganymede."

"What's on Ganymede?" asked Lucky coldly. As far as he knew, there was little or nothing on Ganymede to interest anyone. It was Jupiter's largest moon, but the very nearness of Jupiter made it difficult to maneuver space-ships, so that space travel in its vicinity was unprofitable.

"Tell him," said Henree.

"Look," said Conway. "Here it is. We knew Hansen was important. The reason we didn't have him under tighter observation, the reason Gus and I weren't there ourselves, was that two hours before the pirate attack a report came in from the Council to the effect that there was evidence that Sirian forces had landed on Ganymede."

"What kind of evidence?"

"Tight-beam sub-etheric signals had been penetrated. It's a long story, but the nub of it was that, more by accident than by anything else, a few scraps of code were picked up. The experts say it's a Sirian code and certainly there isn't anything Terrestrial on Ganymede that's capable of putting out signals in a beam *that* tight. Gus and I were going to take Hansen and return to Earth when the pirates attacked, and that's it. Right now we've still got to return to Earth. With Sirius on the scene there may be war at any time."

Lucky said, "I see. Well, before we go to Earth, there's one thing I would like to check on. Do we have motion pictures of the pirate attack? I'm supposing the defenses of Ceres weren't so disorganized that pictures weren't taken?"

"They've been taken. How do you expect them to help?"

"I'll tell you after I've seen them."


Men in the uniform of the fleet, and wearing high-rank insignia, projected the top-secret motion pictures of what later became known in history as the "Ceres Raid."

"Twenty-seven ships attacked the Observatory. Is that right?" asked Lucky.

"Right," said a commander. "No more than that."

"Good. Now let's see if I have the rest of the facts straight. Two of the ships were accounted for during the fight and a third during the pursuit. The remaining twenty-four got away, but you have one or more shots of each of them in retreat."

The commander smiled. "If you're implying that any of them landed on Ceres and are still hidden here, you're quite wrong."

"As far as those twenty-seven ships are concerned, perhaps. But three more ships *did* land on Ceres and their crew attacked the Massey Air-lock. Where are the pictures of those?"

"Unfortunately we didn't get many of those," admitted the commander uncomfortably. "It was a case of complete surprise. But we have pictures of them in retreat, too, and we showed you those."

"Yes, you did, and there were only two ships in those pictures. Eyewitnesses reported three as having landed."

The commander said stiffly, "And three took off and retreated. There's eyewitness evidence of that also."

"But you have pictures of only two?"

"Well . . . yes."

"Thank you."

Back in the office Conway said, "Now what was that all about, Lucky?"

"I thought Captain Anton's ship might be in an interesting place. The motion pictures proved it was."

"Where was it?"

"Nowhere. That was what was interesting. His ship is the one pirate ship I would recognize, yet no ship faintly similar took part in the raid. This is strange because Anton must be one of their very best men or they wouldn't have sent him out after the *Atlas*. Or it would be strange if the truth wasn't that thirty ships attacked Ceres and we had pictures of only twenty-nine. The missing thirtieth was Anton!"

"I could figure that out too," said Conway. "What of it?"

Lucky said, "The attack on the Observatory was a feint. That's admitted even by the defending ships, now. It was the three ships that attacked the air-lock that were important and they were under Anton's command. Two of those ships joined the rest of the squadron in their retreat, a feint within a feint. The third ship, Anton's own, the only one we didn't see, continued on with the main business of the day. It left on an entirely different trajectory. People saw it lift into space but it veered off so radically that our own ships, chasing the main body of the enemy with all its might, never even caught it on film."

Conway said unhappily, "You're going to say that it's going to Ganymede."

"Doesn't it follow? The pirates, however well organized, can't attack Earth and its dependencies on their own. But they *can* put up an excellent diversionary fight. They can keep enough Terrestrial ships patrolling the endless asteroid belt to allow Sirian fleets to defeat the remainder. On the other hand, Sirius can't safely conduct a war eight light years away from their own planet unless they can count on major help from the asteroids. After all, eight light years amounts to forty-five trillion miles. Anton's ship is speeding to Ganymede to assure them of that help and to give the word to begin the war. Without warning, of course."

"If only," muttered Conway, "we could have stumbled on their Ganymede base sooner."

"Even with the knowledge of Ganymede," said Henree, "we would not have known the seriousness of the situation without Lucky's two trips into asteroid territory."

"I know. My apologies, Lucky. Meanwhile we have very little time to do anything. We'll have to strike at the heart instantly. A squadron of ships sent to the key asteroid Lucky has told us of—"

"No," said Lucky. "No good."

"Why do you say that?"

"We don't want to start a war, even if it's with a victory. That's what *they* want to do. Look here, Uncle Hector, the pirate, Dingo, might have burned me down right there on the asteroid. Instead, he had orders to set me adrift in space. For a while I thought that was to make my death look like an accident. Now I feel it was intended to anger the Council. They were going to broadcast the fact they had killed a Councilman, not hide it, goading us into a premature attack. One of the reasons for the Ceres Raid might have been to insure an added provocation."

"And if we do start the war with a victory?"

"Here on this side of the Sun? And leave Earth on the other side stripped of important units of the fleet? With Sirian ships waiting at Ganymede, also on the other side of the Sun? I predict that it would be a very costly victory. Our best bet is not to start a war, but to prevent one."

"How?"

"Nothing will happen until Anton's ship reaches

Ganymede. Suppose we intercept him and prevent the meeting."

"Interception is a long chance," said Conway doubtfully.

"Not if I go. The *Shooting Starr* is faster and has better Ergometrics than any ship in the fleet."

"*You* go?" cried Conway.

"It would be unsafe to send fleet units. The Sirians on Ganymede would have no way of being certain an attack wasn't heading their way. They'd have to take counteraction and that would mean the very war we're trying to avoid. The *Shooting Starr* would look harmless to them. It would be one ship. They'd stay put."

Henree said, "You're overeager, Lucky. Anton has a twelve-hour head start. Even the *Shooting Starr* can't make that up."

"You're wrong. It can. And once I catch them, Uncle Gus, I think I can force the asteroids into surrender. Without them Sirius won't attack and there'll be no war."

They stared at him.

Lucky said earnestly, "I've come back twice now."

"Each time by half a miracle," grumbled Conway.

"The other times I didn't know what I was tackling. I had to feel my way. This time I do know. I know exactly. Look, I'll warm up the *Shooting Starr* and make the necessary arrangements with the Ceres Observatory while that's taking place. You two can get on the sub-ether to Earth. Get the Co-ordinator to——"

Conway said, "I can take care of that, son. I've been dealing with government affairs before you were born. And Lucky, *will* you take care of yourself?"

"Don't I always, Uncle Hector? Uncle Gus?"

He shook hands warmly and whirled away.


Bigman scuffed the dust of Ceres disconsolately. He said, "I've got my suit on. Everything."

"You can't go, Bigman," said Lucky. "I'm sorry."

"Why not?"

"Because I'm taking a short cut to get to Ganymede."

"So what? What kind of a short cut?"

Lucky smiled tightly. "I'm cutting through the Sun!"

He walked out on to the field toward the *Shooting Starr*, leaving Bigman standing there, mouth open.

# 14

## To Ganymede via the Sun

A three-dimensional map of the Solar System would have the appearance of a rather flat plate. In the center would be the Sun, the dominant member of the System. It is *really* dominant, since it contains 99.8% of all the matter in the Solar System. In other words, it weighs five hundred times as much as everything else in the Solar System put together.

Around the Sun circle the planets. All of them revolve in nearly the same plane, and this plane is called the Ecliptic.

In traveling from planet to planet space-ships usually follow the Ecliptic. In doing so they are within the main sub-etheric beams of planetary communication and can most conveniently make intermediate stops on the way to their destination. Sometimes, when a ship is interested in speed or in escaping detection, it veers away from the Ecliptic, particularly when it must travel to the other side of the Sun.

This, Lucky thought, might be what Anton's ship was intending to do. It would lift up from the "plate" that was the Solar System, make a huge arc or bridge above the Sun, and come down to the "plate" on the other side, in the neighborhood of Ganymede. Certainly Anton must have started in that direction, or the defending forces on Ceres wouldn't have missed filming him. It was almost second nature for men to make all spationautical observations along the Ecliptic first of all. By the time they thought of turning away from the Ecliptic, Anton would have been too far away for observation.

But, thought Lucky, the chances were that Anton would *not* leave the Ecliptic permanently. He might have started out as though that would be the case, but he would return. The advantages in a return would be many. The asteroid belt extended completely about the Sun, in the sense that asteroids were evenly distributed all the way around. By keeping within the belt Anton could remain among the asteroids all the way to within a hundred million miles or so of Ganymede. This would mean security for him. The Terrestrial government had virtually abdicated its power over the asteroids and, except for the routes to the four large rocks, government ships did not penetrate the area. Moreover, if one did, Anton would always be in the position of being able to call for reinforcements from some nearby asteroidal base.

Yes, thought Lucky, Anton would remain in the belt. Partly because he thought this, and partly because he had his own plans, Lucky lifted the *Shooting Starr* out of the Ecliptic in a shallow arc.

The Sun was the key. It was the key to the entire System. It was a roadblock and a detour to every ship man could build. To travel from one side of the

System to another, a ship had to make a wide curve to avoid the Sun. No passenger ship approached closer than sixty million miles, the distance of Venus from the Sun. Even there, cooling systems were imperative for the comfort of the passengers.

Technical ships could be designed to make the trip to Mercury, the distance of which from the Sun varied from forty-three million miles in some parts of its orbit to twenty-eight million in others. Ships had to hit it at the furthest region of its retirement from the Sun. At closer than thirty million miles various metals melted.

Still more specialized ships were sometimes built for close-by solar observation. Their hulls were permeated by a strong electric field of peculiar nature which induced a phenomenon known as "pseudo-liquefaction" in the outermost molecular skin. Heat reflection from such a skin was almost total, so that only a tiny fraction penetrated into the ship. From outside such ships would appear perfect mirrors. Even so, enough heat penetrated to raise the temperature within the ship above the boiling point of water at distances of five million miles from the Sun, the closest recorded approach. Even if human beings could survive such a temperature, they couldn't survive the short-wave radiation that flooded out of the Sun and into the ship at such distances. It could kill anything living in seconds.

The disadvantage of the Sun's position with respect to space travel was obvious in the present instance, in which Ceres was on one side of the Sun while Earth and Jupiter were almost diametrically opposed on the other side. If one was in the asteroid belt, the distance from Ceres to Ganymede was about one billion miles. If the Sun could be ignored and a ship could cut straight across space through it, the distance would be only six hundred million miles, a saving of about forty per cent.

This, as far as was possible, Lucky intended to do.

He drove the *Shooting Starr* hard, virtually living in his g-harness, eating and sleeping there, feeling the pressure of acceleration continuously. He gave himself only fifteen minutes' respite out of each hour.

He passed high above the orbits of Mars and Earth but there was nothing to see there, not even with the ship's telescope. Earth was on the other side of the Sun, and Mars was at a position nearly at right angles to his own.

Already the Sun was at its normal size as seen from Earth and he could view it only through the most strongly polarized visiplates. A little more and he would have to use the stroboscopic attachments.

The radioactivity indicators began to chuckle occasionally. Within Earth's orbit the density of short-wave radiation started to reach respectable values. Inside Venus's orbit special precautions would have to be taken, such as the wearing of lead-impregnated semi-space-suits.

I, myself, thought Lucky, would have to do better than lead. At the approach to the Sun that he would have to make, lead would not do. Nothing material would do.

For the first time since his adventure on Mars the previous year Lucky drew out of a special pouch glued to his waist, the flimsy, semitransparent object obtained from the Martian energy beings.

He had long since abandoned any effort at speculation as to the method by which the object worked. It was the development of a science that had continued for a million years longer than the science known to Mankind and along alien paths. It was as incomprehensible to him as a space-ship would be to a cave man, and as impossible to duplicate. But it worked! That was what counted!

He slipped it on over his head. It molded itself to his skull as though it carried a strange life of its own, and as it did so, light gleamed out all over him. Over his body it was a glimmer like a billion fireflies, and it was for that reason that Bigman referred to it as a "glimmer shield." Over his face and head it was a solid sheet of brilliance that covered his features entirely, without, on the other hand, preventing light from reaching his eyes.

It was an energy shield, designed by the alien Martians for Lucky's needs. That is, it was impervious to all forms of energy other than that required by his body, such as a certain intensity of visible light and a certain amount of heat. Gases penetrated freely, so that Lucky could breathe, and heated gases, in passing, were robbed of their heat and came through cool.

When the *Shooting Starr* passed the orbit of Venus, still heading in toward the Sun, Lucky put on his energy shield permanently. While he wore it, he would not be able to eat or drink, but the enforced fast would not last for more than a day, at the outside.

He was now traveling at a terrific speed, far greater than any he had previously experienced. In addition to the slugging pull of the hyperatomics of the *Shooting Starr,* there was the unimaginable attraction of the

Sun's giant gravitational field. He was traveling at millions of miles an hour now.

He activated the electric field that rendered the outer skin of the ship pseudo-liquid and was grateful, as he did so, for the foresight that had made him insist on that accessory during the building of the *Shooting Starr*. The thermocouple which had been registering temperatures above one hundred degrees began to show a drop. The visiplates went dark as metal shields passed over the thick glassite to keep them from damage and from softening in the heat of the Sun.

By the time Mercury's orbit was reached the radiation counters had gone completely mad. Their chatter was continuous. Lucky placed a glimmering hand over their windows and their noise stopped. Down to the hardest gamma rays the radiation penetrating and filling the ship was stopped by the resistance of the insubstantial aura that surrounded his body.

The temperature, which had reached a low of eighty, was climbing again, despite the mirror skin of the *Shooting Starr*. It passed one hundred fifty and still went up. The gravimetrics indicated the Sun to be only ten million miles away.

A shallow dish of water, which Lucky had placed upon the table, and which had been steaming for an hour past, was now bubbling outright. The thermocouple reached the boiling point of water, two hundred and twelve degrees.

The *Shooting Starr*, whipping about the Sun, was now five million miles away. It would approach no closer. Actually it was inside the outermost wisps of the most rarefied portion of the Sun's atmosphere, its corona. Since the Sun was gaseous through and through (though most of it was a gas the like of which could not exist even under the most extreme laboratory conditions on Earth), it had no surface, and its "atmosphere" was part of the very body of the Sun. By going through the corona, then, Lucky was, in a way, going through the Sun, as he had told Bigman he would.

Curiosity tugged at him. No man had ever been this close to the Sun. No man, perhaps, ever would again. Certainly, any man who did, could not look at the Sun with his unaided eyes. The shortest possible glimpse of the Sun's tremendous radiation at that distance would mean instant death.

But he was wearing the Martian energy shield. Could it handle solar radiation at five million miles? He felt he ought not take the chance and yet the impulse tugged desperately at him. The ship's chief visiplate was outfitted with a stroboscopic outlet-series, one which would expose, one by one, each of a series of sixty-four outlets to the Sun, each for a millionth of a second every four seconds. To the eye (or to the camera), it would seem a continuous exposure, but actually any given piece of glass would only get one four-millionth of the radiation the Sun was emitting. Even that required specially designed, nearly opaque lenses.

Lucky's fingers moved remorselessly, almost without conscious volition, to the controls. He could not bear the thought of losing the chance. He adjusted the plate direction toward the Sun, using the gravimetrics as indicators.

Then he turned his head away and plunged the

contact home. A second passed, then two seconds. He imagined an increase in heat on the back of his neck; he half-waited for radiation death. Nothing happened.

Slowly he turned.

What he saw was to stay with him the rest of his life. A bright surface, puckered and wrinkled, filled the visiplate. It was a portion of the Sun. He could not see the whole, he knew, in the visiplate, for at his distance, the Sun was twenty times as wide as it seemed from Earth and covered four hundred times as much of the sky.

Caught in the visiplate were a pair of sunspots, black against the brightness. Threads of glowing white curled into it and were lost. They were heaving areas of activity that moved across the plate visibly as he watched. This was not due to the Sun's own motion of rotation, which, even at its equator, was not more than fourteen hundred miles an hour, but rather to the tremendous velocity of the *Shooting Starr*.

As he watched, gouts of red, flaming gas shot up toward him, dim against the blazing background, and turning a smoky black as it receded from the Sun and cooled.

Lucky shifted the plate, catching a portion of the rim of the Sun, and now the flaming gas (which were the so-called "prominences," consisting of gigantic puffs of hydrogen gas) stood out sharply crimson against the black of the sky. They spread outward in slow motion, thinning and taking on fantastic shapes. Lucky knew that each one of them could engulf a dozen planets the size of Earth, and that the Earth could be dropped into the sunspot he saw without even making a respectable splash.

He closed the stroboscopics with a sudden movement. Even though physically safe, no man could stare at the Sun from that distance without becoming oppressed by the insignificance of Earth and all things Earthly.

The *Shooting Starr* had whipped half around the Sun and was now receding rapidly past the orbits of Mercury and Venus. It was decelerating now. The ship's prow opposed the direction of its flight and its powerful main engines were acting as brakes.

Once past Venus's orbit, Lucky removed his shield and stowed it away. The ship's cooling system strained to get rid of the excess heat. Drinking water was still uncomfortably hot and the canned foods bulged where liquid within had bubbled into gas.

The Sun was shrinking. Lucky looked at it. It was an even, glowing sphere. Its irregularities, its churning spots, and heaving prominences could no longer be seen. Only its corona, always visible in space, though visible on Earth only during eclipses, thrust out in every direction for millions of miles. Lucky shuddered involuntarily to think that he had passed through it.

He passed within fifteen million miles of Earth, and through his telescope he spied the familiar outlines of the continents peeping through the ragged white masses of cloud banks. He felt a twinge of homesickness and then a new resolve to keep war away from the teeming, busy billions of human beings that inhabited that planet, which was the origin of all the men that now occupied the far-flung star systems of the Galaxy.

Then the Earth, too, receded.

Past Mars and back into the asteroid belt, Lucky still aimed at the Jovian system, that miniature solar system within the greater one. At its center was Jupiter, larger than all the other planets combined. About it swung four giant moons, three of them, Io, Europa, and Callisto, about the size of the Earth's Moon, and the fourth, Ganymede, much larger. Ganymede, in fact, was larger than Mercury, and almost as large as Mars. In addition there were dozens of moonlets, ranging from some hundreds of miles in diameter down to insignificant rocks.

In the ship's telescope Jupiter was a growing yellow globe, marked with faintly orange stripes, one of which bellied out into what was once known as the "Great Red Spot." Three of the main moons, including Ganymede, were on one side, the fourth was on the other.

Lucky had been in guarded communication with the Council's main offices on the Moon for the better part of a day now. His Ergometrics probed space with widely stretching fingers. It detected many ships, but Lucky watched only for the one with the Sirian motor pattern which he would recognize with certainty the instant it appeared.

Nor did he fail. At a distance of twenty million miles, the first quiverings roused his suspicions. He veered in the proper direction, and the characteristic curves grew more pronounced.

At one hundred thousand miles, his telescope showed it as a faint dot. At ten thousand, it had form and shape and was Anton's ship.

At a thousand miles (with Ganymede still fifty million miles away from both ships), Lucky sent out his first message, a demand that Anton turn his ship back toward Earth.

At one hundred miles Lucky received his answer —a blast of energy that made his generators whine and shook the *Shooting Starr* as though it had collided with another ship.

Lucky's tired face took on a drawn look.

Anton's ship was better-armed than he had expected.

# 15

## Part of the Answer

For an hour the maneuvers of both ships were indecisive. Lucky had the faster ship and the better, but Captain Anton had a crew. Each of Anton's men could specialize. One could focus and one could release, while a third could control the reactor banks and Anton himself could direct operations.

Lucky, trying to do everything at once and by himself, had to rely heavily on words.

"You can't get to Ganymede, Anton, and your friends won't dare tip their hand by coming out now before they know what's up. . . . You're all through, Anton; we know all your plans. . . . There's no use trying to get a message through to Ganymede, Anton; we're blanketing the sub-ether from you to Jupiter. Nothing can get through. . . . Government ships are coming, Anton. Count your minutes. You don't have many, unless you surrender. . . . Give up, Anton. Give up."

And all this while the *Shooting Starr* dodged through as concentrated a fire as Lucky had ever seen. Nor were all the blasts successfully dodged. The

Shooter's energy stores began to show the strain. Lucky would have liked to believe that Anton's ship was suffering equally, but he himself was aiming few blasts at Anton and landing virtually none.

He dared not take his eyes off the screen. Terrestrial ships, speeding to the scene, would not be there for hours. In those hours, if Anton beat down his energy banks, broke away, and made good headway toward Ganymede, while a limping *Shooting Starr* could only pursue, without catching . . . Or if a pirate fleet suddenly sparkled on-screen . . .

Lucky dared not follow those lines of thought further. Perhaps he had been wrong in not entrusting the interception to government ships in the first place. No, he told himself, only the *Shooting Starr* could have caught Anton still fifty million miles from Ganymede; only the Shooter's speed; more important still, only the Shooter's Ergometers. At this distance from Ganymede it was safe to call in units of the fleet for the kill. Closer to Ganymede and fleet action would have been unsafe.

Lucky's receiver, open all this time, was suddenly activated. Anton's face filled it, smiling and carefree.

"You got away from Dingo again, I see."

Lucky said, "Again? You're admitting he was working under orders in the push duel!"

An energy feeler toward Lucky's ship suddenly hardened into a beam of disruptive force. Lucky moved aside with an acceleration that wrenched him.

Anton laughed. "Don't watch me too closely. We almost caught you then with a lulu. Certainly Dingo was working under orders. We knew what we were doing. Dingo didn't know who you really were, but I did. Nearly from the first."

"Too bad the knowledge didn't help you," said Lucky.

"It's Dingo that it hasn't helped. It may amuse you to know that he has been, shall we say, executed. It's bad to make mistakes. But this kind of talk is out of place here. I'm only plating you to say that this has been fun, but I'll be going now."

"You have nowhere to go," said Lucky.

"I'll try Ganymede."

"You'll be stopped."

"By government ships? I don't see them yet. And there's not one that can catch me in time."

"I can catch you."

"You have caught me. But what can you do with me? From the way you're fighting, you must be the only man on board. If I had known that from the beginning, I wouldn't have bothered with you as long as this. You can't fight a whole crew."

Lucky said in a low, intense voice, "I can ram you. I can smash you completely."

"And yourself. Remember that."

"That wouldn't matter."

"Please. You sound like a space-scout. You'll be reciting the junior scout-patrol oath next."

Lucky raised his voice. "You men aboard the ship, listen! If your captain tries to break away in the direction of Ganymede, I will ram the ship. It is certain death for all of you, unless you surrender. I promise you all a fair trial. I promise all of you the utmost consideration possible if you co-operate with us. Don't let Anton throw your lives away for the sake of his Sirian friends."

"Talk on, government boy, talk on," said Anton. "I'm letting them listen. They know what kind of a trial they can expect and they know what kind of consideration, too. An injection of enzymic poison." His fingers made the quick movements of someone inserting a needle into another's skin. "That's what they'll get. They're not afraid of you. Good-by, government boy."

The needles on Lucky's gravimetrics wavered downward as Anton's ship picked up speed and moved away. Lucky watched his visiplates. Where were the government ships? Blast all space, where were the government ships?

He let acceleration take hold. Gravimetric needles moved upward again.

The miles between the ships were sliced away. Anton's ship put on more speed; so did the *Shooting Starr*. But the accelerative possibilities of the Shooter were higher.

The smile on Anton's face did not alter. "Fifty miles away," he said. Then, "Forty-five." Another pause. "Forty. Have you said your prayers, government boy?"

Lucky did not answer. For him there was no way out. He would have to ram. Sooner than let Anton get through, sooner than allow war to come to Earth, he would have to stop the pirates by suicide, if there were no other way. The ships were curving toward one another in a long, slow tangent.

"Thirty," said Anton lazily. "You're not frightening anyone. You'll look a fool in the end. Veer off and go home, Starr."

"Twenty-five," retorted Lucky firmly. "You have fifteen minutes to surrender or die." He himself, he reflected, had the same fifteen minutes to win or die.

A face appeared behind Anton's in the visiplate. It held a finger to pale, tight lips. Lucky's eyes might have flickered. He tried to conceal that by looking away, then coming back.

Both ships were at maximum acceleration.

"What's the matter, Starr?" asked Anton. "Scared? Heart beating fast?" His eyes were dancing and his lips were parted.

Lucky had the sudden, sure knowledge that Anton was enjoying this, that he considered it an exciting game, that it was only a device whereby he might demonstrate his power. Lucky knew at that moment that Anton would never surrender, that he would allow himself to be rammed rather than back away. And Lucky knew that there was no escape from death.

"Fifteen miles," Lucky said.

It was Hansen's face behind Anton. The hermit's! And there was something in his hand.

"Ten miles," said Lucky. Then, "Six minutes. I'll ram you. By space, I'll ram you."

It was a blaster! Hansen held a blaster.

Lucky's breath came tightly. If Anton turned . . .

But Anton was not going to miss a second of Lucky's face if he could help it. He was waiting to see the fright come and grow. To Lucky, that was plain as could be in the pirate's expression. Anton would not have turned for a much noisier event than the careful lifting of a blaster.

Anton caught it in the back. Death came too suddenly for the eager smile to disappear from his face, and though life left it, the look of cruel joy did not. Anton fell forward across the visiplate and for a moment his face remained pressed there, larger than life-size, leering at Lucky out of dead eyes.

Lucky heard Hansen's shout, "Back, all of you. Do you want to die? We're giving up. Come and get us, Starr!"

Lucky veered the direction of acceleration by two degrees. Enough to miss.

His Ergometers were registering the motors of approaching government ships strongly now. They were coming at last.

The screens on Anton's ship were glowing white as a sign of surrender.


It was almost an axiom that the fleet was never entirely pleased when the Council of Science interfered too much in what they considered to be the province of the military. Especially so when the interference was spectacularly successful. Lucky Starr knew that well. He was quite prepared for the admiral's poorly hidden disapproval.

The admiral said, "Dr. Conway has explained the situation adequately, Starr, and we commend you for your actions. However, you must realize that the fleet has been aware of the Sirian danger for some time now and had a careful program of its own. These independent actions on the part of the Council can be harmful. You might mention that to Dr. Conway. Now I have been requested by the Co-ordinator to co-operate with the Council in the next stages of the fight against the pirates, but," he looked stubborn, "I cannot agree to your suggestion that we delay an attack on Ganymede. I think the fleet is capable of making its own decisions where battle and victory are concerned."

The admiral was in his fifties and unused to consulting on equal terms with anyone, let alone a youngster of half his age. His square-cut face with its bristly gray mustache showed it.

Lucky was tired. The reaction, now that Anton's ship had been taken in tow and its crew in custody, had set in. He managed, however, to be very respectful. He said, "I think that if we mop up the asteroids first, the Sirians on Ganymede will automatically cease being a problem."

"Good Galaxy, man, how do you mean 'mop up.' We've been trying to do that for twenty-five years without success. Mopping up the asteroids is like chasing feathers. As for the Sirian base, we know where it is, and we have a good notion as to its strength." He smiled briefly. "Oh, it may be hard for the Council to realize this, but the fleet is on its toes as well as they are. Perhaps even more so. For instance, I know that the power at my command is enough to break their strength on Ganymede. We are ready for the battle."

"I have no doubt that you are and that you can defeat the Sirians. But the ones on Ganymede are not all the Sirians there are. You may be ready for a battle, but are you ready for a long and costly war?"

The admiral reddened. "I have been asked to cooperate, but I cannot do so at the risk of Earth's safety. I can under no conditions lend my voice to a plan which involves dispersing our fleet among the asteroids, while a Sirian expedition is in being in the Solar System."

"May I have an hour?" interrupted Lucky. "One hour to speak with Hansen, the Cerean captive I had brought aboard this ship just before you boarded, sir?"

"How will that help?"

"May I have an hour to show you?"

The admiral's lips pressed together. "An hour may be valuable. It may be priceless. . . . Well, begin, but quickly. Let's see how it goes."

"Hansen!" called Lucky without taking his calm eyes from the admiral.

The hermit entered from the bunk room. He looked tired, but managed a smile for Lucky. His stay on the pirate ship had apparently left his spirits unmarked.

He said, "I've been admiring your ship, Mr. Starr. It's quite a piece of metal."

"Look here," said the admiral, "none of that. Get on with it, Starr! Never mind your ship."

Lucky said, "This is the situation, Mr. Hansen. We've stopped Anton, with your invaluable help, for which I thank you. That means we've delayed the start of hostilities with Sirius. However, we need more than delay. We must remove the danger completely, and as the admiral will tell you, our time is very short."

"How can I help?" asked Hansen.

"By answering my questions."

"Gladly, but I've told you all I know. I'm sorry that it turned out to be worth so little."

"Yet the pirates believed you to be a dangerous man. They risked a great deal to get you out of our hands."

"I can't explain that."

"Is it possible that you have a piece of knowledge without being aware of it? Something that could be deadly for them?"

"I don't see how."

"Well, they trusted you. By the information you yourself gave me, you were rich; a man with good investments on Earth. Certainly you were much better off than the average hermit. Yet the pirates treated you well. Or at least they didn't mistreat you. They didn't rifle your belongings. In fact, they left your very luxurious home completely in peace."

"Remember, Mr. Starr, I helped them in return."

"Not very much. You said that you allowed them to land on your rock, to leave people there sometimes and that's about all. If they had simply shot you down, they could have had that and your quarters as well. In addition, they would not have had to worry about your becoming an informer. You eventually did become one, you know."

Hansen's eyes shifted. "That's the way it was, though. I told you the truth."

"Yes, what you told me was true. It wasn't the whole truth, however. I say that there must have been a good reason for the pirates to trust you so completely. They must have known that it meant your life to go to the government."

"I told you that," said Hansen mildly.

"You said that you had incriminated yourself by helping the pirates, but they trusted you when they first arrived, *before* you had begun helping them. Otherwise they would have blasted you to begin with. Now, let me guess. I'd say that once, before you became a hermit, you were a pirate yourself, Hansen, and that Anton and men like him knew about it. What do you say?"

Hansen's face went white.

Lucky said, "What do you say, Hansen?"

Hansen's voice was very soft. "You are right, Mr. Starr. I was once a member of the crew of a pirate ship. That was a long time ago. I have tried to live it down. I retired to the asteroids and did my best to be dead as far as Earth was concerned. When a new group of pirates arose in the Solar System and entangled me, I had no choice but to play along with them.

"When you landed, I found my first chance to leave; my first chance to take the risk of facing the law. Twenty-five years had passed, after all. And I would have in my favor the fact that I had risked my life to save the life of a Councilman. That was why I was so anxious to fight the pirate raiders on Ceres. I wanted to make another point in my favor. Finally, I killed Anton, saving your life a second time, and giving Earth a breathing space, you tell me, in which a war may be prevented. I was a pirate, Mr. Starr, but that's gone, and I think I've evened the score."

"Good," said Lucky, "as far as it goes. Now do you have any information for us that you didn't mention before?"

Hansen shook his head.

Lucky said, "You didn't tell us you were a pirate."

"That was irrelevant, really. And you found out for yourself. I didn't try to deny it."

"Well, then let's see if we can find anything else which you won't deny. You see, you still haven't told the whole truth."

Hansen looked surprised. "What remains?"

"The fact that you've never stopped being a pirate. The fact that you are a person that was only mentioned once in my hearing, and that by one of Anton's crewmen shortly after my push-gun duel with Dingo. The fact that you are the so-called Boss. You, Mr. Hansen, are the mastermind of the asteroid pirates."

# 16

## All of the Answer

Hansen jumped out of his seat, and remained standing. His breath whistled harshly through parted lips.

The admiral, scarcely less astonished, cried, "Great Galaxy, man! What is this? Are you serious?"

Lucky said, "Sit down, Hansen, and let's try it on for size. Let's see how it sounds. If I'm wrong, there'll be a contradiction somewhere. It begins with Captain Anton, landing on the *Atlas*. Anton was an intelligent and capable man, even if his mind was twisted. He mistrusted me and my story. He took a trimensional photograph of me (that wouldn't be hard, even without my noticing) and sent it to the Boss for instructions. The Boss thought he recognized me. Certainly, Hansen, if you were the Boss, that would follow, because as a matter of fact, when you saw me face to face later, you *did* recognize me.

"The Boss sent back a message to the effect that I was to be killed. It amused Anton to do that by sending me out in a push-gun duel with Dingo. Dingo was given definite instructions to kill me. Anton admitted that in our last conversation. Then, when I

166

returned, with Anton's word that I was to be given a chance to join the organization if I survived, you had to take over yourself. I was sent to your rock."

Hansen burst out, "But this is mad. I did you no harm. I saved you. I brought you back to Ceres."

"So you did, and came along with me, too. Now it had been my idea to get into the pirate organization, learn the facts from within. You got the same idea in reverse and were more successful. You brought me to Ceres and came yourself. You learned how unprepared we were and how we underestimated the pirate organization. It meant you could go ahead at full speed.

"The Ceres Raid makes sense now. I imagine you got word to Anton somehow. Pocket sub-etherics are not unheard of and clever codes can be worked out. You went up the corridors *not* to fight the pirates but to join them. They didn't kill you, they 'captured' you. That was very queer. If your story were true, you would have been a dangerous informer to them. They should have blasted you the moment you came within range. Instead they did not harm you. Instead, they put you on Anton's flagship and took you with them to Ganymede. You weren't even bound or under surveillance. It was perfectly possible for you to move quietly behind Anton and shoot him down."

Hansen cried, "But I did shoot him. Why in the name of Earth would I have shot him if I were who you say I am?"

"Because he was a maniac. He was ready to let me ram him rather than back down or lose face. You had greater plans and had no intention of dying to soothe his vanity. You knew that even if we stopped Anton from contacting Ganymede, it would mean only a delay. By attacking Ganymede afterward, we would provoke the war anyway. Then by continuing your role as hermit, you would eventually find a chance to escape and take on your real identity. What was Anton's life and the loss of one ship compared with all that?"

Hansen said, "What proof is there to all this? It's guesswork, that's all! Where's the proof?"

The admiral, who had been looking from one to the other through all of this, bestirred himself. "Look here, Starr, this man's mine. We'll get whatever truth is in him."

"No hurry, Admiral. My hour isn't up. . . . Guesswork, Hansen? Let's go on. I tried to get back to your rock, Hansen, but you didn't have the co-ordinates, which was strange, despite your painstaking explanations. I calculated out a set of co-ordinates from the trajectory we had taken going from your rock to Ceres, and those turned out to be in a forbidden zone, where no asteroids could be in the ordinary course of nature. Since I was certain that my calculations were correct, I knew that your rock had been where it was *against* the ordinary course of nature."

"Eh? What?" said the admiral.

"I mean that a rock need not travel in its orbit if it's small enough. It can be fitted with hyperatomic motors and can *move out of its orbit like a space-ship.* How else can you explain an asteroid being in a forbidden zone?"

Hansen said wildly, "Saying so doesn't make it so.

I don't know why you're doing this to me, Starr. Are you testing me? Is it a trick?"

"No trick, Mr. Hansen," said Lucky. "I went back for your rock. I didn't think you'd move it far. An asteroid that can move has certain advantages. No matter how often it is detected, its co-ordinates noted and its orbit calculated, observers or pursuers can always be thrown off by movement out of the orbit. Still, a moving asteroid runs certain risks. An astronomer at a telescope, happening to observe it at the time, might wonder why an asteroid should be moving out of the Ecliptic or into a forbidden zone. Or, if he were close enough, he would wonder why an asteroid should have reactor exhaust glow at one end.

"You had already moved once, I imagine, to meet Anton's ship part way so that I could be landed on your rock. I was certain you would not move very far so soon after. Perhaps just far enough to get into the nearest cluster of asteroids for camouflage purposes. So I returned and searched among the asteroids nearest at hand for one that was the right size and shape. I found it. I found an asteroid that was actually a base, a factory, and storehouse all at once, and on it I heard the sound of giant hyperatomics perfectly capable of moving it through space. A Sirian importation, I think."

Hansen said, "But that wasn't *my* rock."

"No? I found Dingo waiting on it. He boasted that he had had no need to follow me; that he knew where I was heading. The only place to which he knew I was heading was your rock. From that I conclude that one and the same rock had your living quarters at one end and the pirate base at the other."

"No. No," shouted Hansen. "I leave it to the admiral. There are a thousand asteroids the size and shape of mine, and I'm not responsible for some casual remark made by a pirate."

"There's another piece of evidence that may sound better to you," said Lucky. "On the pirate base was a valley between two outcroppings of rock; a valley full of used cans."

"Used cans!" shouted the admiral. "What in the Galaxy has that to do with anything, Starr?"

"Hansen discarded his used cans into a valley on his own rock. He said he didn't like his rock to be accompanied by its own garbage. Actually he probably didn't want it surrounding his rock and advertising it. I saw the valley of the cans when we were leaving his rock. I saw them again when I approached the pirate base. It was the reason I chose that asteroid to reconnoiter and no other. Look at this man, Admiral, and tell me whether you can doubt that I have the truth."

Hansen's face was contorted with fury. He was not the same man. All trace of benevolence was gone. "All right. What of it? What do you want?"

"I want you to call Ganymede. I'm sure you conducted previous negotiations with them. They'll know you. Tell them that the asteroids are surrendering to Earth and will join us against Sirius if necessary."

Hansen laughed. "Why should I? You've got me, but you haven't got the asteroids. You can't clean them out."

"We can, if we capture your rock. It has all necessary records on it, hasn't it?"

"Try and find it," said Hansen, hoarsely. "Try to

locate it in a forest of rocks. You say yourself it can move."

"It will be easy to find," said Lucky. "Your valley of cans, you know."

"Go ahead. Look at every rock till you find the valley. It will take you a million years."

"No. Only a day or so. When I left the pirate base, I paused just long enough to burn the valley of cans with a heat beam. I melted them and let them freeze back into a bumpy, angled sheet of fresh, gleaming metal. There was no atmosphere to rust or corrode them, so its surface remains just like the metal-foil goal posts used in a push-gun duel. It catches the Sun and sends reflections glittering back in tight beams. All Ceres Observatory has to do is quarter the heavens, looking for an asteroid about ten times as bright as it should be for its size. I had them begin the search even before I left to intercept Anton."

"It's a lie."

"Is it? Long before I reached the Sun, I received a sub-etheric message that included a photograph. Here it is." Lucky drew it out from under the blotter on the desk. "The bright dot with the arrow pointing to it is your rock."

"Do you think you're frightening me?"

"I should be. Council ships landed on it."

"What?" roared the admiral.

"There was no time to waste, sir," said Lucky. "We found Hansen's living quarters at the other end and we found the connecting tunnels between it and the pirate base. I have here some sub-etherized documents containing the co-ordinates of your main subsidiary bases, Hansen, and some photographs of the bases themselves. The real thing, Hansen?"

Hansen collapsed. His mouth opened and hopeless sobbing sounds came out.

Lucky said, "I've gone through all this, Hansen, to convince you that you've lost. You've lost completely and finally. You have nothing left but your life. I make no promises, but if you do as I say, you may end up by at least saving that. Call Ganymede."

Hansen stared helplessly at his fingers.

The admiral said with stunned anguish, "The Council cleaned out the asteroids? They've done the job? They haven't consulted the Admiralty?"

Lucky said, "How about it, Hansen?"

Hansen said, "What's the difference now? I'll do it."


Conway, Henree, and Bigman were at the spaceport to greet Lucky when he returned to Earth. They had dinner together in the Glass Room on the highest level of Planet Restaurant. With the room's walls made of curving, clear one-way glass, they could look out over the warm lights of the city, fading off into the level plains beyond.

Henree said, "It's fortunate the Council was able to penetrate the pirate bases before it became a job for the fleet. Military action wouldn't have solved the matter."

Conway nodded. "You're right. It would have left the asteroids vacant for the next pirate gang. Most of those people there had no real knowledge that they were fighting alongside Sirius. They were rather ordinary people looking for a better life than they had been experiencing. I think we can persuade the government to offer amnesty to all but those who had actually participated in raids, and they weren't many."

"As a matter of fact," said Lucky, "by helping them continue the development of the asteroids, by financing the expansion of their yeast farms, and supplying water, air, and power, we're building a defense for the future. The best protection against asteroid criminals is a peaceful and prosperous asteroid community. That way lies peace."

Bigman said belligerently, "Don't kid yourself. It's peace only till Sirius decides to try again."

Lucky put a hand to the little man's frowning face and shoved it playfully. "Bigman, I think you're sorry we're short one nice war. What's the matter with you? Can't you enjoy a little rest?"

Conway said, "You know, Lucky, you might have told us more at the time."

"I would have liked to," said Lucky, "but it was necessary for me to deal with Hansen alone. There were important personal reasons involved."

"But when did you first suspect him, Lucky? What gave him away?" Conway wanted to know. "The fact that his rock had blundered into a forbidden zone?"

"That was the final straw," admitted Lucky, "but I knew he was no mere hermit within an hour after meeting him. I knew from that time on that he was more important to me than anyone else in the Galaxy."

"How about explaining that?" Conway sank his fork into the last of the steak and munched away contentedly.

Lucky said, "Hansen recognized me as the son of

Lawrence Starr. He said he had met Father once, and he must have. After all, Councilmen get no publicity and a personal greeting is necessary to explain the fact that he could see the resemblance in my face.

"But there were two queer angles to the recognition. He saw the resemblance most clearly when I grew angry. He said that. Yet from what you tell me, Uncle Hector, and you, Uncle Gus, Father hardly ever got angry. 'Laughing' is the adjective you usually use when you talk about Father. Then, too, when Hansen arrived on Ceres, he recognized neither of you. Even hearing your names meant nothing."

"What's wrong with that?" asked Henree.

"Father and you two were always together, weren't you? How could Hansen have met Father and not you two? Met my father, moreover, at a time when he was angry and under circumstances which fixed his face so firmly in Hansen's mind that he could recognize me from the resemblance twenty-five years later.

"There's only one explanation. My father was separated from you two only on his last flight to Venus, and Hansen had been in at the kill. Nor was he there as an ordinary crewman. Ordinary crewmen don't become rich enough to be able to build a luxurious asteroid and spend twenty-five years after the government's raids on the asteroids building a new and bigger organization from scratch. He must have been the captain of the attacking pirate ship. He would have been thirty years old then; quite old enough to be captain."

"Great space!" said Conway blankly.

Bigman yelled indignantly, "And you never shot him down?"

"How could I? I had bigger affairs at hand than squaring a personal grudge. He killed my father and mother, yes, but I had to be polite to him just the same. At least for a while."

Lucky lifted a cup of coffee to his lips and paused to look down at the city again.

He said, "Hansen will be in the Mercury Prison for the rest of his life, which is better punishment really than a quick, easy death. And the Sirians have left Ganymede, so there'll be peace. That's a better reward for me than his death ten times over; and a better offering to the memory of my parents."

# Isaac Asimov

| | | | |
|---|---|---|---|
| ☐ | BEFORE THE GOLDEN AGE, Book I | C2913 | 1.95 |
| ☐ | BEFORE THE GOLDEN AGE, Book II | Q2452 | 1.50 |
| ☐ | BEFORE THE GOLDEN AGE, Book III | 23593-9 | 1.95 |
| ☐ | THE BEST OF ISAAC ASIMOV | 23653-6 | 1.95 |
| ☐ | BUY JUPITER AND OTHER STORIES | 23062-7 | 1.50 |
| ☐ | THE CAVES OF STEEL | Q2858 | 1.50 |
| ☐ | THE CURRENTS OF SPACE | 23507-6 | 1.50 |
| ☐ | EARTH IS ROOM ENOUGH | 23383-9 | 1.75 |
| ☐ | THE END OF ETERNITY | 23704-4 | 1.75 |
| ☐ | THE GODS THEMSELVES | X2883 | 1.75 |
| ☐ | I, ROBOT | Q2829 | 1.50 |
| ☐ | THE MARTIAN WAY | 23158-5 | 1.50 |
| ☐ | THE NAKED SUN | 22648-4 | 1.50 |
| ☐ | NIGHTFALL AND OTHER STORIES | 23188-7 | 1.75 |
| ☐ | NINE TOMORROWS | Q2688 | 1.50 |
| ☐ | PEBBLE IN THE SKY | 23423-1 | 1.75 |
| ☐ | THE STARS, LIKE DUST | 23595-5 | 1.75 |
| ☐ | WHERE DO WE GO FROM HERE?—Ed. | X2849 | 1.75 |

**Buy them at your local bookstore or use this handy coupon for ordering:**